STEALING FROM ANGELS

Brian Dullaghan

D1712826

iUniverse, Inc.
New York Lincoln Shanghai

$14.40 may '05

Stealing from angels

Copyright © 2004 by Brian Dullaghan

iUniverse books may be ordered through booksellers or by contacting:

iUniverse
2021 Pine Lake Road, Suite 100
Lincoln, NE 68512
www.iuniverse.com
1-800-Authors (1-800-288-4677)

ISBN: 0-595-33957-3

Printed in the United States of America

For Justin

"There are only two ways to live your life. One as though nothing is a miracle, the other as though everything is."

—*Albert Einstein*

The Prologue

4am. My wife's voice was calm and to the point. I had taken these early morning calls before but somehow I knew that this would be the last one. I dressed and set off on empty roads that were hidden beneath a light Melbourne fog. As I approached Saint Benedict's I slowed down, signed the cross and said a prayer out loud for little Justin. I set the heating to high and turned the radio on just in time to hear a woman describing her empty life now that her husband of 50 years had passed away. The radioman let her talk without interruption. Near the centre of town I saw some vagrants in a park huddled under useless blankets and I wondered what could have destroyed these people's lives.

The hospital was peaceful, the buzz of a failing fluorescent and the slap of a wet mop the only distractions. I made my way to the cardiac ward on the 7th floor and saw my wife waiting near the entrance. We didn't speak. The two nurses attending to Justin looked at me with a terrible sadness. Both moved away as I approached. His body was so tiny. His condition for almost all of his short life had prevented proper feeding. The heart specialist arrived and after standing with us for a few moments called me to one side. He told me that my son was about to die. I was asked to give approval to withdraw all medical support and let nature take its course.

9am. I remember some guy handing me a business card and saying, "our rates are good." He must have lived in the hospital waiting for people to die. Maybe someone from the hospital contacts him and he pays them a commission or a spotter's fee. Death is a business. Funeral directors look dead. This guy must have weighed 50 kilos, dripping wet. He had a noticeable lean in an attempt to seem apologetic—trying to secure my business while at the same time, comforting me. Still, I took the business card. I even gave him the gig, eventually. I also met with a young female counsellor who put her arm around me saying, "It is for the best…really." She came out of nowhere. Maybe she was hiding behind the dead man. She was slight. Maybe they were a team. I think I frightened her. I just stared. She must have been barely eighteen. Work experience perhaps. Learning how to tell someone it's, 'all better now,' when the one person in the world you loved has gone. I won the staring contest and she slowly backed away, head bowed. She slid backwards along the corridor as though she was on roller blades but she had enough stamina to give me one last defiant look. What did she want me to say anyway? 'Yes dear, you are right. Justin is much better off not experiencing the joys and pleasures of life, far better to die at the age of seven and a half months before having to deal with shaving everyday.' I saw a priest lurking in the hallway but he must have sensed it was not a good time to introduce himself. The only genuine comment I remember was from the doctor who had attended to my son near the end. As we left the 7th floor of the Royal Children's Hospital he touched me on the shoulder and said, "I will miss him too." The head nurse had given us a few minutes in private before they took his body to the morgue. We used that time to wash and dress Justin. I brushed and then cut a small lock of his hair. When the nurse and her assistant returned, we left.

We made our way out of the hospital to join the Friday morning chaos and waited patiently for the intersection lights to change. The world was its normal self. Inside cars women applied new coats to their faces and businessmen fumbled with ties. The light changed and we crossed over heading for the park opposite. We found a bench, sat down and didn't speak a word for what seemed like an hour. People walked by saying "morning" or nothing at all. A group of school children paraded in front of our bench each taking a peek at the two totally forlorn characters seated there. I can't remember who spoke first. "We'd better make arrangements then," one of us suggested. The other agreed. We sat for another thirty minutes or so before I stood up. I walked forwards a little so that I could get a better view of the 7th floor, the Royal Children's cardiac wing. Last window on the right. A family one minute, then just the two of us. Eventually my wife stood and joined me. She asked me if I could see the room. I pointed it out. She looked towards the hospital following my outstretched arm, and began to cry. It seemed impossible that she had any tears left. She buried her face in her hands and sobbed. I don't know how to describe my own feelings. I had no emotion and every emotion at once. I had the presence of mind to walk her back towards the road and although I had driven in that morning I hailed a cab. The driver took little notice of us and in no time we were home. I paid the cab fare while my wife let herself in, not seeing the changes I had made to the garden.

I entered the hallway just in time to see my wife walk into the nursery. I stood at the doorway and watched as she picked up a teddy that was lying on its side in the cot. She gently propped it up, took another stuffed toy from the other end of the cot, and placed it alongside. The Mr. Men curtains were untidy so they were pulled closed and then re-opened. Now they were even. She stood in the centre of the room and did a final inspection before turning to walk back out again. I told her I would make a cup of tea and went off to the kitchen. I thought about making something to eat but doubted she'd be able to eat anything. I'd been living alone for several months while my wife stayed in temporary accommodation next to the hospital. This was mainly for convenience, and because Melbourne was in the grip of a nurse's strike which forced parents to help out with general duties. For the most part I lived on takeaway so I couldn't have offered her more than a slice of toast.

I was filling the kettle when I heard a noise like a bump. I turned off the tap and listened again. It was quiet. I replaced the kettle and walked into the hallway only to find my wife lying on the hallway floor seemingly unconscious. The muscles in my stomach pulled tight. For a moment I couldn't figure out what had happened. I couldn't breathe and I just stared at her. Everything rushed at me. I felt Justin's last breath again. Then it hit me. I had agreed to turn off the life support to my own son. I felt giddy. I ran to the bathroom and threw myself at the sink. I vomited so much I almost collapsed. I slid down against the bath and cried my heart out.

I was still sprawled out when I heard a murmur coming from the hallway. I had forgotten all about my wife. We were like two battle weary fighters recovering from a stoush. I dragged myself into the hallway to attend to her. She asked me where Justin was. I sat alongside of her, held her close and told her he was safe.

Doctor Copland, our family doctor, arrived only minutes after my call. He explained that my wife was in shock. He was worried that I might be in shock too and gave us both medication. The lady next door came over, having seen Doctor Copland leave, and sat with my wife, who was now lying on our bed. Our neighbour was a nurse and a great friend to both of us. I left the girls alone and loafed around the house. I went into the kitchen and made some toast but I couldn't eat it. I poured myself a glass of water took a few sips and went back to the bedroom. I stood at the door and watched as Joan comforted her. She was holding her hand and speaking to her in a very soft, caring voice. My wife was nodding but I couldn't hear anything of the conversation.

It was there, leaning against the doorway that I remembered the beautiful lady. As yet I hadn't mentioned anything. I was preparing myself just before that group of school children marched by us in the park. I was going to say something in the cab ride home but my wife had enough to deal with...I would tell her later.

I coughed to attract attention and suggested I might make some tea. They didn't acknowledge me. I went out the back and sat on the verandah and as I looked across the garden, imagined a child running wild. I heard children's laughter across the fence, and realized how painful things were going to be for my wife.

The girls talked for hours, and as I sat alone, I recalled the incredible events in my life that had led me to this point.

CHAPTER 1

We stood outside the building and pretended we were having a smoke break. Shaun had a clipboard under his arm and I was leaning against our trolley. We were told to expect the delivery truck anytime between 9am and 9.30am. It arrived a little after nine. Shaun and I wore baseball caps, which had the name of the company neatly embroidered on the front. The driver pulled up, saw us at the entrance to the building wearing company uniform and checked that we were to collect the delivery for Thomas Lavean and Sons. He opened up the rear door to his truck and handed us two large boxes. Shaun studied the consignment note to check that everything was in order and then signed his name to the delivery slip. The deliveryman waltzed along the side of the truck, climbed in and drove off. With the two boxes on our trolley, we pushed it up the street, placed the boxes into the boot of Shaun's car, and drove off.

That was a sting, a very simple one. My employer wanted the contents of those boxes. They contained files relating to a property development in New York. Thomas Lavean and Sons were the consultants handling the tender for a large government housing scheme. Our boss needed to know the bidding price and any conditions his competitors had specified.

I'd been in New York one month and was working and earning. I was learning a trade. One that would make me a lot of money over the coming years. My friend Shaun Quinn had introduced me to 'the firm.' Quinn had been living in America for around nine months, having arrived from Dublin under similar circumstances to me. Shaun was seen stealing a car in Dublin, ramming it into a jeweller's store and making off with the goods. He knew that the car he stole belonged to the Garda and said that it "added to the occasion." If caught he would certainly have gone to prison, so, like many Irish immigrants before him, he decided to see America with no time to say goodbye to his Mother.

My employer, Lucio Gelli was a man who cut a fine figure in an Italian suit and who couldn't see without his dark sunglasses. I was impressed with Gelli right from the off. The location for our first meeting was a fancy downtown restaurant. It was his birthday. His group, which included most of his New York people and a few foreign associates, had booked the place out. I sat next to a guy who told me he hired extras for movies. I didn't make the connection at the time but Gelli used these people as props for big stings. He would set up a fake office in an empty warehouse and use the extras to fill the role of workers doing general clerical work. The most common use for this elaborate set was related to document handling.

Shaun had mentioned to one of Gelli's men that he had a friend just arrived from Dublin who was very quick on his feet. He was told to bring me along that day to the restaurant and see how I fitted in. Shaun told me to wear my Sunday best because the boss liked to see everyone well turned out. The hoods in Dublin never dressed well. Leather jackets that were two sizes too small, bellbottom jeans, a pullover (in case they got cold) and platform boots to make them look bigger than 160cm, the average height of a Dublin gangster.

Gelli looked like 'the man' and to everyone that worked for him, he was. Shaun had been doing some simple errands for him and Gelli liked his no-nonsense approach to getting the job done. He was mainly being sent out to recover documents for Gelli. This is how Shaun had explained it to me: If Gelli got into a business deal with someone he would want to see their hand before playing his own. If a DA were harassing him he would want to know what they had on him. If Gelli were taking over a business (or a racket of some kind) he would want to see the real books, the real profit margins, before making a deci-sion. Basically, if he wanted to blackmail someone, he would ask Shaun to find the necessary hook. There was much more to it than this but Shaun was a bit naïve. Not that I wasn't. This was where I found my niche, working for Gelli.

The firm worked out of an eight storey building on the edge of the CBD. The business occupied the entire 1st floor and offered two separate entrances. One entrance was via the building's lobby and lift, and the other was via a direct access door at the top of a flight of stairs, which led from the rear park-ing area. The layout of the floor included several offices, two meeting rooms, and an apartment style boardroom, which had private shower and toilet facili-ties. There was a reception area, waiting room, and a home kitchen. The recep-tionist, Olivia, whom I saw socially a couple of times in my first year, told me that she would take dozens of calls an hour from Gelli's associates, all of whom had several companies under their control. In the main lobby there was a list of all the companies operating out of the building. They included legal firms, financial advisors, developers and consultants of every variety. There were more firms listed as trading from the 1st floor than all the other floors combined.

I was originally told that the firm's day-to-day business was primarily sales and distribution of products relating to the building industry. Overall it looked to me like a normal place of business. I never heard the firm referred to by any single business name and I didn't know if any of the regular 1st floor people were really involved in the sales or distribution of anything. The office side of Gelli's business seemed legitimate but then there was the other side, which operated outside normal hours and collected data for the firm and its many associated companies. For this, a different set of qualifications was required. Gelli had big guys to do the rough stuff but he needed small skinny guys who could climb walls and shimmy through narrow windows into private offices around the city. It was important that his errand boys could read, to ensure that the correct documents were recovered. Sometimes stealing a document required nothing more than waiting outside the main entrance of an office and accepting the mail. Looking inconspicuous was a key requirement in the job description. Accepting the mail or packages just delivered was something I would do many times in my first year. I was born for this work. I had been relieving people of their private property since I was six years old when I used to visit relatives' houses and sell them their own watches. One uncle of mine bought his own watch three times.

Gelli seemed to like me first up. He was impressed enough with young Shaun and I assume he believed all the things Shaun had said about me, most of which would have been grossly exaggerated. Shaun had not been employed directly by Gelli. He had met one of Gelli's men while hanging around a pool hall. The man had asked Shaun if he wanted some work and Shaun, who had been mainly shoplifting for income to that point, said he did. Working for Gelli was no ordinary nine to five job. Sometimes we wouldn't hear from anyone for weeks. Then, without warning, one of his hoods would come around to our hotel and pick us up with, "Come meet the Boss, he has a job needs doin." Gelli didn't like black people, but he wasn't one to let personal prejudice interfere with business. He needed people that knew the streets, knew the scene. He didn't think much of the Jews either. I overheard him speaking to a man who was visiting from South America that first day at his birthday party.

They were speaking about the war when Gelli said, "It's a pity the trains weren't longer, you would have gotten rid of all the bastards." They laughed and others standing nearby joined in. It was many years later before I understood the depth of his bigotry.

I was enjoying America. Shaun and I were making some good money, mainly in chunks when we pulled off a job, but we were both cautious and made what we had last. New York was not the place to be poor. Everything was so expensive compared to Ireland, especially accommodation. This could be well over half what you would earn in a 'normal' job. By the end of the first year I thought of Gelli as a broker. None of the documents we stole related to him. He headed up a large ring of executives who all needed to be bailed out of something at some time or another. They were a brotherhood of sorts and all members of a group called the Freemasons. Gelli was a proud Italian American and it was common knowledge that he held no regard for Catholicism. Gelli asked me once if I was a Catholic and for my opinion of the church. I told him all the priests I'd known were alcoholics and that I could never understand why the only decent buildings in Cabra were churches. I said I would never steal from a church as a sign of respect for my father, who had a very high regard for all things Catholic.

In all the time I knew or worked for Gelli I only met with him directly about a dozen times. Most of these meetings, at least six, came in my last year with him. By then I could speak his language. It appeared that he wanted some initial personal contact with his team but after that you heard little from him. He had various people who handled different aspects of the work. You would come under their management and that was whom you reported to. Shaun and I did our jobs and didn't ask too many questions. We liked being considered hoods and New York was our town. Really we were just two pratts from Dublin who would do well to feck off home.

I felt fortunate to have a job and I respected Gelli because he was providing me work. He had also personally secured my work permit. I didn't really know enough back then to form an opinion of the man. I think, had I known about his background, it wouldn't have changed anything. I wanted my crack at the big time as I saw it.

I had come to America after some old school friends of mine decided to step up in class and rob a bank. I had nothing to do with the group by this stage but I was implicated. I had barely seen these guys since I'd left school, as I preferred to tread the criminal road alone. I always felt that a crook was less likely to get caught if they acted alone. One of the lads had been clocked during the robbery and the police very quickly extracted the names of his associates. The Dublin police have a great record for solving local crime. The poor bastard probably gave me up under the stress of a severe beating, which led to a search of my house. My older sister tipped me off. I actually thought they were after me for a scam I was running at the time but didn't wait around to ask questions. If the Garda were after you it was a good time to take a holiday. I was lucky that I had a current passport having gone on a packaged holiday the previous year with my ex-girlfriend. It was the only time I had left Ireland and I was very unsettled after getting back. Things always look great when you're on your holidays. I said then that I would leave Ireland. My girlfriend retorted that I couldn't go to the end of the street on my own. I wished I'd gone on that holiday on my own. She was either too hot or the food was crap and much to her disgust the beaches were full of half naked women; another reason why I wished I'd gone on my own. I had a bit of money put away and this got me a ticket to America with enough to live on for a few months. Being Irish, I didn't need a visa, which was a relief, as I hadn't thought to get one.

I was surprised that Shaun had kept in touch after he went over. Shaun was a bit of a fragile chap and I think he must have been lonely when he arrived in New York. He probably decided to write to everyone he knew in the hope of getting a response. He was an only child, which in Ireland is about as rare as having two heads. Standing only 160cm tall Shaun was better suited to being a jockey than any other profession. His high-pitched voice and his 60 kilo frame were never going to frighten anyone into handing over their hard-earned wedge. He would have struggled to have any life in Dublin because he had such a disliking for the police there. The car he took was not the first thing he'd stolen from the Garda. When we were kids Shaun was forever giving cops the finger and calling them names. This would always end up with us running for our lives. It was only after reminding him about this in America, during one of our long 'an-do-ya-remember' talks, that I began to understand his hatred. He told me that the police had once wrongfully accused his father of a serious crime. They had almost beaten him to death in order to gain a confession out of him. Clearly, Shaun would have continued to wage his personal war with the Garda had he stayed at home, eventually shooting one of them or being shot himself (the most likely outcome).

So Shaun and I were making our way in New York. We found a local drinker with Irish beer on tap and told grand tales to the other expatriates who longed to hear stories of home. Exaggeration is an important tool in the Irishman's vocabulary. Telling a story is a sport in Ireland. The winner is the one who can tell the most bullshit without losing the interest of the audience. Often the stories begin with a simple recollection of an event that you may have overheard. Sometimes you may actually be recounting the story of an incident that really happened to you but this would be rare. As the ale flows and the night dies, the audience becomes impatient, and with that grows a need to up the ante with lies or embellishments. It is then, and only then, that the true Irish storyteller comes into his own. I have seen pubs near closing suspended in silent animation as all about the bar listen to a man tell the riveting tale of the labourer who fell fourteen floors only to be saved by a freak gust of wind, a wheelbarrow and a bag of sand. Most of the things I know today as fact are stories I overheard that could never be true.

CHAPTER 2

I was born in Cabra, one of seven children, which for the time and geography, was considered a rather small family. We were a close-knit group, which came more from living in a two-bedroom house than any saintly desire to get along. However, we survived and I have great memories of my childhood. It was a time when you could leave the key in your door and have people dropping in for tea. But things changed, especially when people like Shaun and I realized that everyone left their key in the door.

We spent most days playing cards in the gutter outside Jimmy Web's house. You could sit and play in the gutter in those days because no one had a car. In fact, I would become the first to have a car in my street but I couldn't bring it home for obvious reasons.

I lived on a long road where the houses all looked the same. It's a wonder the drunks could find their way home. Our front yard was six feet deep with a little brick fence. The house was one window and one door wide. The back garden was a massive twelve feet by the width of the house. Inside we had a good room, a kitchen, and a little back room. Upstairs we had two bedrooms, a box room, and a bathroom. We had bunk beds that were three beds high. If you slept on the top bunk your nose touched the ceiling. If you slept on the bottom bunk you were in danger of being crushed by the top two. I slept in the middle. I didn't know that we were poor because everyone else had as little as we did. We didn't go hungry and there was always a fire burning in the good room. My life was filled with friends and a family that loved me. You couldn't want for anything else.

One of my best memories is the football. We had magnificent games of football in a park just round the corner. Sometimes twenty a side and forget forty-five minutes each way, these games lasted for days. It wasn't unusual for the match to be still going at 10 o'clock at night. When it got dark we'd just say, "ok then it's 56 to 55 and we'll see ya here in the morning." The idea was not to lose, so once you got ahead the ball would miraculously go missing or you'd start a fight. At 8 o'clock the next day everyone would roll up for the next world championship.

When we weren't playing cards or football we would be in the picture house after entering through the exit. Entering through the exit takes a lot of skill. One of us would go in to see a film by the conventional manner—that is we would actually buy a ticket. The person who paid would suddenly have a need to spend a penny. The exit was inside a corridor, which housed the little boys' room so you could open the exit and let your mates in. That left one small problem. One kid goes into the toilet and eleven kids come out. One at a time was the key and keep low. Girls had no sense of humour when it came to bunking in to the pictures, as we called it. When my big brother and I had our first double date we decided to go to the pictures to see a Carry-on film. The picture house was always a good place to feel out the potential of a new girlfriend. I suggested that the girls go around to the exit and wait for me to let them in but they told me to feck off and went home. My brother told me not to worry, "they're bikes anyway," meaning that anyone could ride them. Anyone except me and my brother.

The Cabra slops lorry was a weekly highlight for me and my friends. Your man would come around each Thursday and collect the potato peelings and other scraps, which he then sold to the piggery round the back of our place. We would climb up into the tray at the back and help level the leftovers so the fella could pick up more slops. It was great fun and we stank for days.

At the end of my street was a grand church. The attached school was where my education began. Books were replaced with a slate roof tile referred to as a personal blackboard and our writing implements, naturally, consisted of chalk. As well as feeding my brain, the school also provided me with dinner. A school dinner is something put on for those poor unfortunates who had no packed lunch or whose mothers banned them from walking the hundred or so paces home for lunch. The food was not related to gourmet and the menu Monday through Friday was Irish stew. Take it or leave it. We had nothing to compare our lives to and our lot was our lot.

We had our share of sad times. There was always someone dying in Cabra. You could barely go more than a few months without having to put on your Sunday best and head for the graveyard. I guess it's because all the families were so large, it was only natural that this increased the death rate. Drink also increased the death rate but rarely got a mention at any service I attended. The Irish have an unusual way of celebrating the passing of a loved one. We call it the Wake. Providing it's not a tragedy such as the death of a child, the dead person's family puts on a party with a decent spread. I liked funerals for this reason. I remember my Granda's funeral (on my Mother's side). The coffin had been laid out in the middle of the good room on a couple of trestles and the lid was removed so that everyone could say their last good-byes. I remember my Granny giving the dead man a pillow and me thinking how stupid that was. I couldn't see the point in my Granda wearing his best suit but there he was. The food was all laid out but not to be touched until we got back from the funeral. I thought that was a bit unfair. Granda was going to miss his own party. I went over to the spread, made up a lovely plate and put it on Granda's chest, as he lay there asleep. I then went outside to see if any of my mates were around. Suddenly there was this loud scream coming from the house, loud enough to wake the poor bastard. My Granny had gone over to say her very last good-byes to her husband of some sixty years when she saw a cheese and tomato sandwich hanging out the side of his mouth. My Dad killed me for doing that. The story however has since become a favourite amongst our relatives. I was only six at the time.

My mother was always very sick during my childhood and eventually died after having been slowly murdered by Doctor Miller the local GP. He started the killing in March of 1963 when he first prescribed her Valium. She had complained of 'not quite feeling herself' after having one of the girls. He continued to prescribe Valium to her on every visit, which ranged from bouts of the flu, sore legs to a series of bad headaches. "Valium is what you need, there you go." Miller had my mother addicted to the drug. He introduced other drugs to help offset the damage of being on three Valium a day for fifteen years. Eventually, my mother was taking pills to offset the effect of these 'other' pills that she couldn't even remember being prescribed. None of us knew that this wild cocktail had been going on for so long. Such was the health service of the time. Everyone in the waiting room got Valium no matter what the ailment. Miller could put two-dozen women through his surgery in an hour. When my mother died she was in her mid fifties but looked over a hundred. After her death members of the family started to question the cocktail of medication that was only now coming to light. Spent tablet bottles were turning up everywhere. Miller even gave pills to my sisters on mum's behalf. If she were too ill to go and see him, one of the girls would run down to the surgery to make an appointment for a house call. His response, "give her these, if she doesn't feel better tomorrow come back and I'll give you something else to try." The lazy bastard wouldn't make a house call until you were dead.

Sadly I was not around when Mum died but I heard a nice story about how her older brother went to see the good doctor and killed him, but he only took a few minutes. My uncle was a great character. His passion was gambling, the dogs mainly and the occasional horse race. A friend in a pub gave him his first dog. The dog's name was Blacky and he was grey. The friend no longer wanted the dog because he was such a handful, keeping neighbours awake with his rowdy behaviour and so on. The only way Blacky could have disturbed the neighbours was with his snoring. My uncle invited us kids down to the green to watch his first training session. He headed off on his bike with a lovely bit of steak hanging off the back. I was to hold the dog and let go when I heard the whistle. The whistle went, I let go of the dog, and we all had steak and chips for tea.

Not deterred by the obvious lack of form shown by Blacky my uncle pursued the dog trainer career and eventually got a few dogs with ability. He soon learned the tricks of the trade. He would go along to a small meeting and just before sticking the dog in the starter box he would shove a dollop of treacle into his mouth. The gate opened and the dog flew out. After the first bend, the dog would try to suck in some air but the magic treacle would block his airway. He would suddenly run out of puff and finish last. After two or three meetings the treacle wasn't required and the dog would fly home at great odds. My uncle spent half his life watching his dogs run and the other half running from disgruntled bookies.

My Dad had done his very best to turn us into God fearing children. We all attended church. Somehow though, we all went in search of other gods. Some of the seven children returned while others have hedged their bets, changing camps in line with different levels of grief. I had the occasion to see which camp I belonged to after the death of a loved one left me looking for answers. Religion is funny that way. It's like when people win the lottery they have this burning need for a new car or house but when people lose money they have this burning desire for Jesus. Despite his best efforts, my father had something that he was ultimately unable to teach or instil in us children, and that was faith. He told us all the great stories from the Bible and other great tales of miracles and holy men. One of his favourites was the story of Padre Pio.

On September 20, 1918, Padre Pio was kneeling in front of a large crucifix when he received the visible marks of the crucifixion. The doctor who examined Padre Pio could not find any natural cause for the wounds. These wounds, which neither healed nor festered, were still bleeding at the time of his death, fifty years later. The wounds of the stigmata were not the only mystical phenomenon experienced by Padre Pio. Many people claim to have received miracle cures from the humble priest. When he died on September 23, 1968 at the age of eighty-one, about 100,000 people attended his funeral.

I heard this story a hundred times or more. It was mandatory telling on special occasions such as Saturdays, Sundays and any other day that someone appeared in our good room. Like the time I was sitting on the lounge with my girlfriend Sarah having a good old snog. I thought that Dad, along with everyone else, was out at a church fair but in he pranced, sat in 'his' chair and proceeded to tell her about Padre Pio. There we were, Sarah with her pantyhose halfway down her thighs and me with a would-be woody, listening to a story about a guy with holes in his hands. You had to be there.

Dad's need to tell these stories repeatedly was an exercise in re-charging his faith. Yet, despite this obvious outpouring of affection for all things religious he would find time to make the worst jokes, poking fun at these same institutions. His favourite joke involved a couple that he had met on one of his many pilgrimages to Lourdes. There on the afternoon of February 11, 1858 a fourteen year old girl named Bernadette Soubirous, while collecting firewood on the banks of the Gave de Pau, claims to have seen a vision of Our Lady. Separated from her sister and a friend, Bernadette said that she heard a great noise, which she described as like that of a huge storm. Turning toward the source of the noise, a nearby grotto known as Massabielle, Bernadette claims she saw a rosebush being blown by the wind, but the air, she says, was still that day. Curious, intrigued, even frightened, Bernadette moved closer to the grotto. As she did, a golden cloud appeared out of the opening. From that cloud appeared a beautiful lady, dressed in white with a blue ribbon and roses on her feet. The woman, described as sixteen or seventeen years of age, wore a veil and held a rosary of white beads with a golden chain. It soon became apparent to Bernadette that the lady was the Virgin Mary. Instructed by the Blessed Virgin to dig into the earth at the grotto, Bernadette discovered an underground stream whose waters would soon become known throughout the world for their healing powers. Catholics from around the globe visit this spring in the hope that they may be cured of life threatening illnesses.

My Dad was partial to a dip in the magical spring waters of Lourdes and it was here that he met the butt of one his all time favourite jokes. My dad had been asked to help push a man through the holy water as his wife was too old and frail to do so. The wheelchair bound man had not walked for years being crippled with multiple sclerosis. He would tell the story with great pride and have people on the edge of their seats awaiting the news that he had witnessed a great miracle in the holy springs of Lourdes. My dad would describe how he and the man waited patiently in line before he pushed the heavy, squeaking wheelchair down into the spring, through and out the other side. "Well…well," people would ask in anticipation, "was he cured?" Dad would reply, "oh no, but the wheelchair never squeaked again." Everyone would piss themselves. How could such a religious man take the mickey out of such things?

My Father and I share a great (or terrible) affliction and that is the ability to take people off. I use the word affliction because we don't seem to be able to stop ourselves once the occasion arises. When I was at school I could take off the actions of any teacher or schoolmate. Dad was the same and when we were together no one and no thing was sacred. Taking the piss out of people was a way of life in Dublin. You made your own entertainment.

Our home was filled with great relics from Dad's crusades. I had everything from original splinters of the cross carried by Jesus of Nazareth, to small fragments of clothing from various Saints, including our very own patron Saint Patrick, under my pillow. Saint Patrick was a great one for chasing snakes. Ireland never really had snakes and no one can agree on who Saint Paddy really was. The latest bet is that he was French. That would make sense because there are plenty of frogs in Ireland. I always enjoyed receiving the gifts, even holy water, but I never took any of them to be authentic.

As a young boy, having already begun my career in relieving people of personal effects, I appreciated the potential earnings from selling such items. As a child I could only wonder at how big the cross, carried by the Son of God, must have been. The church has been selling parts of this artifact for a thousand years or more. There used to be an advertisement in the Irish Times for 'Cross of Nazareth splinters.' Underneath the advert was written, 'wholesale inquiries welcome.' As for the bits and pieces of cloth worn by the great saints this always seemed highly unlikely. So many of these people were not even recognized in their own times so why anyone would have retrieved clothing worn by them for future followers to sample is beyond me. Holy water was the best con of all. Millions of litres of holy water housed in receptacles of every kind are sold each year. The Irish love holy water. A teahouse in Kerry used to sell afternoon tea and scones made exclusively with holy water.

Dublin is a grand City that attracts tourists from every nation. I didn't appreciate this much as a kid. We never went much further than the end of the street. Occasionally my parents would take us to the park after Sunday mass. Phoenix Park was great; they have a great Zoo and we used to love teasing the lions by sticking our hands through the wire fence and pulling away just before the lion could bite your hand off. On the way back from the park we would go downtown and walk by the Liffy or climb Nelson's column. There were over a hundred and fifty steps to take before reaching the viewing platform but your efforts were rewarded with a spectacular view of the city. I learned all about our monument to the British Navy hero, Horatio Nelson in school so naturally I can't remember anything of it other than it was in Sackville Street. The locals didn't like the monument and referred to it as, 'an obstruction to traffic' and nobody seemed too disappointed when the IRA blew it up in 1966. Everyone in Dublin has a piece of the column as a souvenir (wholesale inquiries welcome).

Once or twice a month we would go to the market. I loved to see all the vegetables laid out. I hated vegetables but loved to look at them. There were always people selling cheap lighters and cigarettes at the market. They would be pushing a pram and shouting, "cigarettes, five packs for a pound" and when a customer approached them they would reach in to where the baby should be and pull out the stock. I imagine these goods were stolen because if the Garda appeared these people would just vanish. The Moore street market was also great for flowers, hundreds of flowers in every colour. These always fascinated me, because I'd never seen a flower growing in anyone's garden so I wondered where they came from. Apart from the market, the park, and the column, another favourite of mine was looking at doors. The houses are nothing special but I doubt if any city in the world has such magnificent doors. The Georgian houses that surround the city each have a unique doorway. They hold competitions and award prizes to the best door. Streets around Merrion Square in particular attract hundreds of onlookers each weekend, eager to see the pretty painted doors of Dublin. Our door was red.

We went to Trinity College once. My brother and I got lost in the great library. Dad wanted us to see the book of Kells but we wanted to play hide and seek. We hid and dad spent the day looking for us. I don't remember seeing the great book but I have since learned all about this masterpiece created by monks in 800AD. The book was copied by hand and consists of the four gospels Mathew, Mark, Luke, and John. Some of the scrollwork can only be seen with a X10 magnifying glass, (which was not invented until four centuries after the book was completed.) I did some scrollwork once with my penknife in the school toilets; the headmaster knew it was me. I said it was art, like the book of Kells. He said it was shite and made me paint half the school.

The city was alive. I loved to watch the characters pass by as we sat on the steps of the GPO having a sandwich after one of our days out. We never went far without my mother's famous tomato sandwiches. They would be sopping wet by the time we got to eat them and they tasted great.

CHAPTER 3

I was expelled from high school at the age of 14 years and 11 months. I had organized a protest march to take place at the front gate of Cardinal Newman High School at noon. The idea was that the older students, who had some genuine grievances about the way the school was run, would march up the road, make a bit of noise, and that would be that. The whole school went out. I couldn't believe it. I even tried to encourage the younger ones to go back but they were up for it, so off we went. Someone called the local papers and the next thing I knew I had a reporter saying, "now, as the leader what is your main gripe?"

"Oh, I'm not the leader sir," I said, "I thought there was a fire drill!" The next day I got my marching orders without the chance to say goodbye to my school friends many of whom I would never see again.

The day after I was expelled my dad took me out to one of the new industrial estates and suggested I 'cold' call on the factories and see how I go. He wasn't disappointed that I had left school so early because the family needed another income. My older brother and sister were both working and paying board and I wanted to make my contribution towards the cost of running the house. I got a job the same day working in a plastic factory that made wallets and carry bags and other useless items. I impressed the supervisor with my previous work experience. I had been working in the local chipper since I turned thirteen. The job was five nights a week and it paid quite well. I had to pour big sacks of potatoes into a peeling machine and then tidy them up after they fell out into a big tub. I would have my hands in icy cold water for two hours a night as I washed and picked off the little bits missed by the automatic peeler. When I was finished I was allowed a bag of chips and a bottle of soft drink so it was OK really. I only stopped working there a few weeks before I got expelled from school. The owner had a heart attack while putting a basket of fish in the big fryer. He fell in headfirst—it was a terrible sight. His wife closed the business down and put the shop on the market.

The plastic factory was a good start to my working career. It was a fair way from home though, which was a real bastard in the winter. I had an area to myself at the rear of the factory where I operated the machines that cut up the plastic sheeting. I could play my radio and generally goof around. I also got the odd flash of knicker from one of the office girls who worked on a mezzanine level built at the front of the factory. Miriam O'Reilly had a great arse and most days started with a good look at it. She knew I could see her as she bent over to pick up files that for some reason were always stacked on the floor, instead of her desk. She often tried to catch me looking up at her. I perfected the art of looking up whilst looking down. It put a terrible strain on my eye muscles doing that all day. Anyway, Miriam had been poked more times than a second-hand dartboard so I restricted our relationship to voyeurism.

I soon got involved in ordering materials and preparing quotes for the sales rep. The sales guy couldn't tie his own shoelaces and relied on me to accurately quote material needed for jobs. I made sure he bunged me a few quid from his commission each month. I was also suggesting ways the company could improve its efficiency with better job schedules and improved use of the off cuts for smaller jobs. I had a feel for this business thing.

I was earning a living, paying my way at home and had started my first romance. She was a great girl and her mum was a great cook. They had a color TV so I was well away. Her dad was a carpenter and I used to work weekends with him for extra cash. He helped me get my first motorbike and taught me how to do basic repairs. So now I had everything, including wheels.

I worked in this one place for two years and tried hard to save and get ahead but there was always something to spend money on. Having a girlfriend didn't help. It meant everything you did cost twice as much. I never bunked her into the pictures, though I did think of it a few times. I used to love bombing around on my motorbike but I kept falling off. I think the seat must have been loose or maybe it was the wheels. One night, after being over at the girlfriend's house, I had a terrible accident. It had been raining and I was approaching a bend not far from my house. Just as I hit the bend, a bus came out of nowhere and I had to swerve to avoid colliding with it. The front wheel of the bike hit the large curb and threw me over the handlebars. Just as I crashed into a wall headfirst, the bike decided to land on me. I was lying there when this cobshite came out of the house and told me off for damaging his brick fence. I had to pick up the bike and push it home. Another time I was flying down a cutting after being out in the country when a large bird flew out of the bushes and jammed itself in my front wheel sending me arse-over-head. I had several visits to hospital thanks to that shagging bike.

I wasn't ungrateful, what with the job, me girl, and transport. But I wanted more. I could see that working nine-to-five with a bit of overtime would only get you so far. I was doing all the work and all the boss was doing was Miriam. A group of friends I used to hang out with, were going up in the world much faster than I was. They had cars and were living in their own flats, a real sign of success. However, none of them had jobs and they certainly weren't living this lifestyle on the brew (dole). These lads had formed a team to rob places: the post office, a warehouse, and eventually a bank. I can report that this was their last job, for a while anyway. It gave me to thinking. Shaun Quinn was doing OK and he'd never done a day's work in his life. He was selling goods that he found in warehouses. I bought my first stereo from Shaun for five pounds. They were seventy pounds in the shops so you had to be in. How could I make some money, real money? I didn't like the idea of stealing goods because it meant hard work, lugging boxes all over the place and trying to hide the goods from the Garda. I stole a car once with my friend Trevor Connelly. He could really drive and we had some great weekends tearing around, but we couldn't park the car outside either of our houses. We eventually swapped the car for a nylon string guitar. I needed something neat and tidy to make my pile. So, after a long brainstorming session I hatched a brilliant scheme that was to make me a small fortune.

First I needed an ID card, a clipboard, a haircut, and a pen. 'Tele-Rent' was born. "Good morning madam. I'm from Tele-Rent and we have a great offer for you. For only five pounds you can have one of these colour TVs, pictured here, in your home for one full year. All you have to do is pay a deposit of two pounds and the balance on delivery." My strike rate was about twenty percent. On a good day I made a hundred pounds. This was an absolute fortune. I would head off to towns around Ireland spending the nights in local B&B's. I rarely paid for the accommodation, as I'd sign them up too. I threw in the job in the plastics factory and began my new life as an entrepreneur. After a month or so word got around that some shagger was out selling bogus TV rental. Still, I'd made my pile, which helped me start other assorted projects. On a sad note,

my girlfriend left me for a man with a machine that dug holes in the ground. I
told her he was an idiot trying to find Australia. I was sad to break up with her.
I liked her a lot and I really liked being around her family, especially at meal-
time. They had the only set of teacups I'd ever seen with all the handles still
intact. By now the fix was in. I would never again work in a freezing cold factory. It was suits all the way for me.

I became frustrated at life in Dublin and started to look at other possibili-
ties. I used to gaze into the windows of travel agents dreaming of far off places.
America was the one place that always stood out for me. It was natural for Irish
people to head off to America, something we had been doing since it was discovered. Although, I could never understand how you could 'discover' a place
that already had people living there when you arrived. The British sent many
an Irishman to America during the great famine. Most people can't understand why the Irish hate the English of that time but the Poms' actions during
this great food shortage was reason enough. The great famine meant nothing
to me as a kid. All I knew was that the potatoes went bad and there was nothing to eat. That couldn't be further from the truth. The potatoes did go bad but
these farmers grew other crops. The landlord (installed by the British) was to
be paid a percentage of each harvest and the family living on the land kept the
rest. During the famine, the landlords took all the other crops as rent leaving
the tenants nothing to eat. The British saw this as a great opportunity to convert the local peasants. "We will give you food if you swear allegiance to the
Crown and denounce your religion." Very few did. On one of my trips back
home in later years I visited a churchyard deep in the potato famine region of
Southwest Ireland. I stood beneath a tree that had a small plaque, which read:
"Here in the ground where you are standing lie the bodies of twelve hundred
children who were buried in an open grave during the first year of the famine."
Having read about the famine as an adult and reading some of the personal letters written at the time by locals, I have acquired a respect for those who still
seek answers from the British. One such letter I will never forget. A man
describes how he was systematically burying his children. This line alone was
enough to move me to tears: "Today we buried Nancy and tomorrow we think
it will be the turn of our youngest Thomas." I never hated the British. I take
people for who they are and how they treat me. Most nations have things in
their past that they wish hadn't happened. Anyway, just like my ancestors, I
had been forced to leave my country. One Garda who had signed up with Tele-

Rent was heard saying, "I will kill that scrawny little bastard if I see him again." That would keep any semblance of homesickness at bay for a while.

CHAPTER 4

My first real assignment for Gelli came in 1971. At this point Shaun and I weren't spending much time together as he had moved out of our hotel to shack up with a girl he'd met from Long Island. I was getting more involved with the firm and operating solo some of the time. I was also doing some operational planning for Gelli's business associates, which meant dealing directly with the customer. I was very quickly gaining a reputation in the city as someone who could be trusted to retrieve important documents. I was also coming to terms with my trade. It was neat and tidy and nobody got hurt. I had the obligatory sunglasses but only wore them on bright sunny days. I was learning all sorts of tricks with a focus to gaining access to buildings. Often the front door was good enough even during business hours. People expected to be robbed of money and jewels but few took precautions with documents. Mostly these documents were minutes of meetings or outlines for court proceedings by DAs and were usually left lying around on the desk or in unlocked filing cabinets. Sometimes critical documents were in safes and Gelli had a man for those jobs.

I was to work with Jimmy Step just a few times but he spent hours teaching me about safes and strong boxes. He introduced me to small explosives and skeleton keys. Jimmy was a classic safe man, a bit nerdy looking with thick, black rimmed glasses and more hair in his eyebrows than atop his head. He was scrawny with long piano player's fingers. He liked to crack his finger joints before showing me a procedure. I hated that sound. I had a friend in Ireland who could attract a crowd to watch him crack various body parts. He used to crack the bones in his neck. It made me shiver. Last I heard he was in a wheelchair.

Acquiring knowledge about a company's security arrangements was easy. Former employees were a good source along with disgruntled security guards who had been given the flick for one reason or another. We always knew what to expect, what tools were required. I spent weeks studying everything there was to know about different types of locks. The key to my work was secrecy, so blowing doors off safes was only a last resort. The longer it took someone to realise a document was missing or had been copied or tampered with, the better. Everything was considered on the job, from fingerprints to leaving a warm light bulb to alert someone to a theft. When police were called to a suspected break-in they would perform a routine series of checks which would indicate if anyone had been in the room and when. It's amazing how many clues a burglar leaves when he commits a robbery. Police estimate that even the most seasoned professionals leave at least two or three clues at a crime scene.

Gelli introduced me to a major crime squad detective who taught me everything he knew about crime scenes. Alain Del-Rosa was with the New York Police robbery squad. Alain had been asked to give me the run down on what to avoid when committing a robbery. I couldn't believe that a man whose job it was to catch crooks was spending time educating me on how to avoid detection. I was invited to spend some time working with Alain on real cases. He mainly worked out of his car. When he wasn't responding to a call or doing paperwork he was parked outside his favourite donut stand. He was a big guy, huge in fact, but likeable. When a call came in he responded quickly and professionally. If asked, I was to say I was a court reporter on work experience. One time we responded to a break-in at a jewellery business on the east side. I don't know why we bothered driving because we could have walked the two miles faster, or at least I could have. The thieves hadn't touched the items in the front retail store, just the gold ingots in the safe. The major crime unit was involved because this was the fourth robbery on a similar type of business in little over a month. The burglary had gone unnoticed until mid-morning when the jeweller opened the safe. We walked around the premises and entered through the main door. Alain had already calculated that there had been at least two robbers. Once inside he pointed out some clues that the robbers had left and indicated that the NY police department was not far away from hauling in some suspects. We walked back to his car, drove off to see Doctor Donut, and had a debriefing session. Alain reeled off half a dozen obvious mistakes the burglars made, whilst eating half a dozen donuts.

I listened intently to Alain as I learned all about clues and how not to leave them behind. Some of the most damming clues a criminal leaves behind are things that may fall out of a pocket. It could be a cigarette butt or an empty gum wrapper, the smallest thing. Alain gave me access to some crime reports, which spoke of the evidence, how it was gathered, and eventually built into a bulletproof case to take to trial. Some of the criminals I read about seemed like honest hard working thieves but some were just plain thick. There was a story about a guy who robbed a rich couple in Manhattan. He had stolen over a hundred grand's worth of stuff including money and personal items. He wore gloves and probably wiped his feet before entering the apartment building. He had taken every precaution but the poor guy must have had too much to eat before committing the crime, and once inside the apartment had to go to the bathroom. The police had a suspect for the robbery thanks to the security guard on duty who had earlier taken down a licence plate number. Seems the guard just didn't like the look of the robber's car parked out front of the building and recorded the plate. The police had no solid clues linking the driver of the vehicle to the robbery until the lady of the house noticed that the en-suite toilet had been used. Turns out the robber had removed his gloves, and when finished washed his hands before wiping everything down. The mistake he had made was picking up and flicking through a glossy magazine whilst sitting on the toilet. His prints were all over it.

Then there was the plain stupid guy. After demanding all the cash from a till a robber asked a liquor store worker to hand over a bottle of scotch that was on a shelf behind him. The worker said, "I can't do that, as I don't believe you are 21." The robber got angry and said, "I am too over 21…here…I can prove it." With this he showed the employee his drivers licence. The employee said, "oh…ok then, here it is." The robber left. The police arrived at his house before he did.

Many of the crime reports were lighthearted but far too many were about gruesome violent murders. They reminded me that I was a very small time hood and God willing would stay that way. I was being primed. Why? I had no baggage that was obvious. I was almost invisible in this great metropolis, which would add a significant amount of time to any police investigation should I make a mistake and leave my calling card behind.

By this time I had met with most other members of the firm and it appeared I was accepted into the fold. I was invited to a number of house parties and was mixing with more and more of the associates for whom I was actually working. It was at such a function, in late 71', that I was introduced to Frank Sturgis.

Meeting Frank and subsequently working with him changed everything for me. Gone was my nice little well paid job that saw me living like a king compared to my life in Dublin. Sturgis was an assassin. He didn't introduce himself that way, it wasn't his title but that's what he was. He fought with Castro then turned against him. He ran several Castro assassination operations, killed many throughout the Americas, and admitted to conducting assassinations in the United States. Whilst working on a job with him in Washington he bragged about being the other JFK shooter—thing is, I believed him. Frank was straight out of a crime show. It's a wonder he could go out in public without being arrested on suspicion of something—anything. He had those, 'I'm guilty' eyes, blank but threatening. He was a heavy man but not overweight. He liked to bob his head like one of those dogs you see in the back of cars. "How's it going Frank?" Bob, bob, bob. I guess that meant ok or, I have no idea how I'm going. I was to help Frank get some information from a man named Ellsberg.

Dr. Ellsberg was working for the US defense department when he decided that he needed a bonus. He offered to leak some documents to the Washington Post, which told of the farce in Vietnam and what the Government really felt about the war. He claimed that he had proof of major contracts being issued without adherence to the normal tender process and implied that he would expose certain Government officials for knowingly supporting such activities. Gelli had many friends at the Post and one such person tipped him off. This war, as it turns out had been good business for most of Gelli's mates as they had interests in companies supplying goods and services to the armed forces. Some of the contracts were worth tens of millions of dollars for everything from weapons to body bags. The good doctor was potentially going to damage the business of these men should he decide to offer this news to a legitimate source such as the Washington Post. Sturgis asked me to recover whatever documents Ellsberg had. I was supplied with some details in relation to the Doctor, his home and known associates and then left to my own devices.

I did the surveillance myself. Coming and going, morning jog, etcetera. I had a large window to work with because the Doc was out for long periods each day. He lived alone and rarely had visitors. Neighbours were the best way to get information about someone. I put on a jacket that had the name of a courier printed over the breast pocket and knocked on his neighbour's door. I chose a house that was two houses away as it would be less likely they were close friends. An elderly woman answered the door. I said I had a package to deliver and could she tell me when the gentleman might be home. In one minute flat I had the life and times of one Doctor Ellsberg who was said to be polite and regular! I had two spotters for the job. These men were provided with a two-way radio and would keep me informed of movements in the street near or around the doctor's house. The Doc had gone to some trouble to hide the files he took from work but I eventually found them. They were marked 'copy only'. It was important that he didn't suspect they had been tampered with or he might publish them sooner. Before touching anything I made a mental record of the entire room. Once I found the files I spent as much time looking at how they were arranged as I did reading and copying them. I made sure that I didn't leave any dents in the paper by picking pieces up and having them fold over in the middle on me. The best way to handle a flimsy bit of paper is to let it fall on the ground or onto a flat surface. The information was quite damning but time permitting, there were enough holes for Gelli to tip off the offenders on both sides and draft bogus contracts. About a month later, the Washington Post published a series of documents leaked to them by Dr. Daniel Ellsberg.

There was no major damage to the firm. Sturgis congratulated me and said he would use me again. On the one hand I was pleased because he was clearly involved with the major league, but on the other I was unsure about working for him. I hadn't seen Gelli for ages so I needed to get more involved with people like Sturgis. You were only paid when you worked. There was no retainer. Gelli actually spent most of his time in Italy where he was managing the same type of operation as he was in the States. Ultimately, he was in everything or should I say his associates were. Most of the business was legitimate; that is, the service or product they provided was legitimate. The way they won their share of the available market was not so legitimate. The firm would get to the people awarding the work, which led to multimillion-dollar projects rolling in from all over the place. In a six-month period, associates of the firm won every major contract they bid for. In some of these cases I had supplied information about competitors final bids using the sting that Shaun had perfected. But mostly the firm had bought someone.

I was uncomfortable around Frank Sturgis. He was a hood through and through. He liked to brag about previous jobs and the great men he had met. He told me a lot of things about my employer, leaving me in no doubt that Gelli was a much bigger player than I had previously thought. Frank told me that Gelli's power reached across America and Italy. He had close ties to the CIA and was collaborating in terrorist activities in Argentina. If Frank had any credibility, Gelli's affairs went much further than I'd ever imagined. Frank lived in Miami and saw himself as a bit of a playboy. I went to his place once after doing some work for a local politician and Frank tried to impress me by having four chicks turn up late at night to party. These girls were charging more per hour than I was. I made out that I was right into it but I didn't get right into anything. Two of the girls made out with Frank on his king sized bed. He was still bobbing his head around as he gave those two girls a right seeing too.

By mid June 72' I would have no need to worry about working with the likes of Frank Sturgis anymore.

CHAPTER 5

During the first half of 72' I was involved with a number of document recoveries and a couple of neat stings. I was getting regular work from various members of the firm and my income was substantial. When I wasn't working I spent time with people like Alain and Jimmy and read books on crime and crime scenes. I had become fascinated with how technical crime can be. The stings we were pulling were nothing compared to some of the elaborate jobs pulled off around the world.

One of my favourites involved a guy who started up his very own financial institution. He offered fantastic interest rates and people abandoned all the other banks to give him their cash. First he leased a building that some years earlier had been the local branch office of a major bank. He invested some money in the project bringing in shop fitters to kit the place out. He came up with the name, Pyramid Building Society and up went the shingle.

His marketing started with flyers that he simply placed on car windscreens in this medium sized town in Australia. His flyer included testimonials from other Pyramid branches around the world with stories of great wealth generation. Opening day arrived and the staff had to contend with hundreds of people trying frantically to give away their life savings. The Society offered 17.5% interest on amounts over 1,000 pounds. The only catch was that you couldn't touch your money for six months. As it turned out you could never touch your money again. Depositors received hand written savings books complemented with an official looking stamp. This was not unusual for the 1960s and in line with the practice adopted by most major banks around the world. It would be difficult, if not impossible to run the same scam today.

That scam was a 10 out of 10 for me. Brilliant work. After four months, the Society sent out a flyer to depositors saying that they were going to be closed for one week in order to increase the size of the branch. They even announced that due to the overwhelming success of Pyramid they were going to open another local branch, which would offer employment to over twenty local people. During the week of the closure, the branch was disassembled. On the first day that the Pyramid office should have re-opened there were a handful of people outside the door. On the second day there were over 10,000 people in the streets demanding answers. Local politicians were threatened with physical violence because they had shown their support for this great new enterprise. The story I read didn't indicate the exact amount of money involved but it reported that many prominent persons were too embarrassed to admit how much they had lost. The staggering thing is, they had no permit to open a shop let alone a bank or building society, which would normally have to be approved by parliament. Everyone in the town assumed that Pyramid must have followed all the correct procedures in establishing such a business. Many criminals regard this sting as one of the all time greats. No arrests were ever made. In June of 1972 I was to get involved in an event that would outrank the great Pyramid saga for fame but for very different reasons.

The June 17 break-in at the offices of the Democratic National Committee was a total cock-up. It became known as Watergate. Five burglars broke into the apartment complex in Washington DC to steal…nothing. To this day no one has supplied a satisfactory explanation for what happened that night or what, if anything, these five burglars were after. There are hundreds of books dedicated to the story of how Richard Nixon, the President of the United States of America, was behind a scheme to spy on and sabotage the Democrats. I don't know if Gelli knew Nixon but I do know the so-called break-in had nothing to do with spying on the Democrats. The continued speculation about Watergate eventually led to Nixon resigning as President. On August 9, 1974, Nixon handed his resignation to the Secretary of State. It read, "Dear Mr. Secretary: I hereby resign the office of President of the United States." Sincerely, Richard Nixon.

The papers of the day reported, "five men, one of whom claims to be a former employee of the CIA (good one Frank), were arrested at 2.30 am yesterday in what authorities described as an elaborate plot to bug the offices of the Democratic National Committee. Three of the men were native-born Cubans and another allegedly trained Cuban exiles for guerrilla activity after the 1961 Bay of Pigs invasion. They were surprised at gunpoint by three plain-clothed officers of the metropolitan police department in a sixth floor office at the plush Watergate building, where the Democratic National party occupies the entire floor." A young guard, Frank Wills first noticed something was wrong when one of the doors connecting a stairwell and the hotel basement garage was jammed open with tape over the lock. The doors all the way up the stairwell to the sixth floor were the same, giving access from the stairwell to the hallway of each floor. There was no immediate explanation as to why the five suspects would want to bug the Democratic Committee offices or whether or not they were working for any individual or organization. A spokesperson for the Democratic Committee said records kept in those offices were not of a sensitive variety although there were some financial records and general Committee papers. Police report that, "two ceiling panels had been removed, which suggests that the place was to be bugged. All suspects were wearing rubber gloves at the time of their arrests." Police also reported that, "the men had $2,300 in cash between them and one walkie-talkie. They also carried a 35mm camera and 40 rolls of unexposed film. Two of the men were captured near the filing cabinets and a National Committee source conjectured that the men were preparing to photograph the contents."

Gelli was absolutely furious about the break in. The court reports were comical. "In court yesterday, one suspect said the men were anti-communists and the others nodded in agreement." One DA described the operation as "professional and clandestine." One of the Cuban natives, the Washington Post reported, is now a locksmith in Miami. Police reported that the tools appeared to be packaged in burglary kits. (Like you can go into K-Mart and buy a burglary kit right next to the fishing equipment!)

The five men Sturgis, McCord, Gonzalez, Barker, and Martinez were working for Gelli. They were guests at the Watergate hotel, sharing two rooms on the fifth floor. They were even observed eating in the main restaurant only the night before their arrest. All five men were released on bond. The reports and conspiracy theories that rained down on the US from this so-called burglary were, and still are, ridiculous.

At one point I was tempted to call a talkback radio show and tell the good people what had really happened but I realized it was more pathetic than Watergate itself. What really happened that night is no longer a story of any interest and the fact that the police never uncovered the real plot, even though it was to happen in the same building, is more reason not to reveal it now.

It was the end of relations between Sturgis and Gelli who was angry, not because the men were caught but because it prevented them from doing the planned job. Gelli lost face with a powerful political figure in Washington, who was conveniently in Chicago that night and the firm lost a lot of money because of the stuff up. Gelli called me, he asked me for my opinion on the events, and said he should have put me in charge of the whole operation. He wasn't serious but I couldn't have done any worse. Sturgis had controlled the operation along with Martin, another associate of the firm. I was a very minor player, becoming involved only when all of the main details had been worked out.

I was told to track the movements of someone who had been living in one of the apartments within the large hotel complex. He resided there under his own name. He wasn't a celebrity but he was a very powerful individual. I monitored his movements for a few days and fed the information back to Sturgis. The key objective to my surveillance was to get a look at this person's diary and give Frank details of any appointments he had made.

Frank was interested in the timing of one particular meeting that was to take place in Washington but not necessarily at the hotel. Breaking into a room at such a complex should have been difficult, but it was easy. In fact I didn't break in I let myself in using a key that I had stolen from the cleaner's trolley. The apartment was set up like a normal small office with a small entertainment area and the normal things you would expect, kitchen, bathroom and sleeping quarters. The apartment had two bedrooms and both were being used. Apart from copying appointment times from the man's diary I read some current mail and flicked through some reports that were either being read or prepared. I updated Frank on everything. He said the information I gave him would help ensure the job was a success. What is it they say about the best laid plans....

I will say this much. A great story of political intrigue exists today because a Cuban, whom Frank had put in charge of making the doors secure, couldn't count or didn't recognize the words fifth floor as being the 5th floor. If the police had done a thorough check of the other people living in the apartments they would have seen another possible scenario.

The Washington Post did its best to get a major story out of it, but the reporters had nothing to work with. There were stories of money having been stolen the week before and bugging devices miraculously appearing all over the place. The items found on the robbers grew, from the ones I've already mentioned to include crowbars, gas masks, automatic firearms, and a helicopter standing in wait in a nearby field. All bollocks the lot of it, but everyone involved made such a hash of things they had to keep the conspiracy theory alive. There was a story about a $25,000 cashier's check previously earmarked for President Nixon's re-election campaign turning up in an account owned by one of the burglars. The papers seized on this as proof. I especially like the story of a 'Mister Big' that was the mastermind behind the 'Real Watergate story.' Endless books have been written about this person. There was no Mr. Big, just Frank.

The officer in charge of the arrest that night informed the five men that they were being arrested for breaking into the offices of the Democratic Party. To this news one of the Cubans was quoted as saying, "what's a Democratic Party?"

CHAPTER 6

After the Watergate debacle I was given more responsibilities within the firm. This included writing job briefs and selecting team members if there was a call for extra men. I was given the use of an office in the firm's building and access to a PA should I require assistance.

I liked living in New York. I used the subway to get around the city and never had any problems using the network despite claims that everyone was mugged at least once on the trains. The city has thousands of cabs but it was quicker to walk to most places. I liked to remind myself how much I'd saved by walking. Even if I got drenched I would still feel chuffed at having saved a few bucks. The other problem with catching a cab was that someone would invariably be opening your door at the other end, which required tipping. Old Jack made his wages from tips he earned opening doors to the firm's visitors, except me. He looked resplendent in tails, more like a CEO than a doorman. He did me for tips as best he could by grabbing anything I was carrying before I had time to say no. He also did his level best to eyeball anything he carried for me, which was another reason I tried to avoid him. I was mindful however to be nice to Jack because I saw Gelli hug him once, as if they were buddies. I was also suspicious that he was related to Olivia. I saw them leave together a couple of times.

I used to play the big 'I am' and keep people waiting before having one of the PAs show them in. I am sure they all thought I was a bit of a tosser but I liked playing the executive from time to time. It was difficult to pull off any job single-handedly but I would exhaust every possibility before including anyone else in an assignment. The more people you included, the greater your chance of failure. Whereas I wouldn't tell anyone what I was doing, not everyone could be trusted to be so careful. Take Watergate for example. One of the burglars had told his wife, "if I haven't called you by 2am please call my room as I might be in trouble." Fact: the men were arrested at 2.30am. A receptionist took a call from someone around 2.15am saying, "can you go check on my husband's room as he is not answering and he said if he wasn't there I should alert some-one." I never assumed that any of the people I worked with were bright. If I had been working with Shaun I would know how careful he was about sticking to the plan. At the hotel in Washington, there were five guys on the sixth floor instead of six guys on the fifth floor, the sixth one being yours truly.

One of the firm's most high profile jobs, which also included a huge pay-check for me, was to find and destroy information that was potentially damag-ing to the re-election aspirations of Juan Domingo Peron.

Peron, who I thought was dead by this time and who had been president of Argentina from 1946-1955, was again running for the top job. Gelli, who had been a friend of Peron's for some years, was asked to help in the election cam-paign. I was surprised when Gelli asked me to get involved as it was in another country but by now I had earned his total trust. The job was suited to my style and I was still a virtual unknown to the authorities. Despite the money and power the friends of the firm had, they couldn't perform the tasks themselves, so I was important in that sense. However, the more I worked for the firm the more I was aware that I knew far too much about their business. This kept me employed but could also be my undoing should I ever be accused of being dis-loyal.

I decided to read a book about Peron on the way to Argentina because I didn't want to appear ignorant if I was asked questions about the former leader during my stay. Peron had a love-hate relationship with the Argentineans that began in the forties when he joined a clique of military plotters who overthrew the ineffective civilian government of Argentina. The military regimes of the following three years came increasingly under the influence of Peron. The future leader had shrewdly requested for himself the minor post of secretary of labor and social welfare. By 1945 he was Vice President and Minister of War. Clearly, he was bidding for undisputed power, based on the support of the underprivileged laborers and on his popularity and authority within the army. In early October 1945, Peron was ousted from his positions by a coup of con-stitutionally minded civilians and officers. He was arrested and placed in cus-tody but his beautiful and dynamic mistress, Eva Duarte and associates in the labour unions, rallied the workers of greater Buenos Aires and Peron was released from custody on October 17. The night he was released he addressed 300,000 people from the balcony of the presidential palace, which was broadcast to the nation on radio. He promised to lead the people to victory in the pending presidential election and to build with them a strong and just nation. A few days later he married Eva, or Evita as she was popularly called, who would help him rule Argentina in the years ahead.

Evita was very popular with the poor of Argentina issuing subsidies and grants to a range of groups. She was responsible for distributing food and clothing to needy families. She pushed for more housing to be made available for the underprivileged, and access to jobs and medical services for all people. She was responsible for the setting up of countless programs, which included hospitals, women's refuge centres, and a nurse's training centre. One of her housing projects provided homes to 25,000 workers. Evita was acclaimed in many countries and afforded movie star adoration while on official visits. In Spain, she received the country's highest decoration: the Great Cross of Isabel the Catholic. Pope Pius XII received her. The gold rosary he gave her would be placed in her hands at the hour of her death. Not all Italians were so welcoming. The Communist Party demonstrated its repudiation of her visit by shouting, "down with Fascism!" There were other protests along the way as the tour continued, but the Communists were the strongest. In France she met the future Pope John XXIII and gave a large donation to the victims injured in the violent explosion, which destroyed the Port of Brest. Evita was also responsible for gaining women the right to vote in Argentina. The Eva Peron foundation, which Evita said was designed to 'bridge the gap,' was the target of controversy in Argentina.

The Foundation's balance sheet for 1953 specifies the origin of its funds: cash donations, mostly from unions but also from individuals and companies, collective bargaining agreements, taxes, rents, legislative grants and so on. Stories circulated about forced donations, where resistance was met with persecution. I was later to learn that these claims were true. This on-going controversy was the nature of my involvement. Peron had advised Gelli that a certain group was threatening to blackmail him and his party with documents proving funds from the foundation were being misused. They were not wrong. I located the documents thanks to intelligence provided to me by an aide who was working for Peron.

I had travelled to Buenos Aires alone while someone at the firm had arranged for a man to collect me at the airport. I can't remember if I was early arriving or my contact was late but I spent a long time in that crowded terminal. The arrival hall and the check-in counters were all lobbed in together. There were groups of people shouting at each other with arms flailing about. Then, just as I thought there was going to be a punch up, they'd start hugging each other. It was hot and I couldn't find a cafeteria anywhere, or a spare seat. The flight had been bad enough, now I just wanted to relax. I had travelled first class and the service was brilliant but the plane had made a God-awful rattling sound the whole way. At one point we hit some turbulence and I thought it was going to fall apart.

Eventually I scored a seat near where I was told my contact would collect me. Diego found me with ease, as I was the only person in the entire terminal not shouting at someone. He welcomed me to his town and we set off for the city. It was a long drive from the airport to the capital and Diego smoked a packet of cigarettes along the way pausing between drags to play tour guide. The city was massive with the usual mixture of poor dwellings and swanky buildings that you'd expect to find in a major city. We arrived at the hotel quite late so I just checked in and went straight to bed. Diego, as it turned out, was also sharing my hotel room. By morning I had full-blown asthma.

I spent a few days surveying the building where the potential blackmailer lived and conducted business. The man involved would have been implicated as much as anyone if the files had been released to the press but he had developed such hatred for Peron that he was prepared to go down with him. I found the original files containing some very damning information resting on the desk of this disgruntled former employee. One of Peron's aides made contact with the man to discuss a financial settlement and during that meeting I broke into his apartment. Peron decided not to use a local man because he didn't know whom he could trust. He didn't have the same power that he had enjoyed back in the forties and fifties.

After taking the documents, I quickly made up a dossier of the potential blackmailer's involvement in misappropriating funds from the foundation established by the beloved Evita. Juan Peron released this dossier to the press. The poor soul couldn't believe what had happened. He couldn't dispute anything because the document I created showed proof of illegal payments received by him that were 100% accurate. I was able to get the evidence against him because Peron had authorized the payments. By the time he figured out who had stolen his original files he was under guard, charged with fraud and in prison.

In the elections of March 1973, Peronist candidates captured the presidency and majorities in the legislature and in June, Peron was welcomed back to

Argentina with wild excitement. In October, in a special election, he was elected back to the top job. It's difficult to say if the information about misuse of funds from the foundation would have damaged his chances at the election but I can say that at a meeting with Gelli shortly after his win, Peron kneeled before him to thank him for his assistance.

I visited Argentina several times over the coming year, most of these trips relating in one way or another to the Eva foundation.

CHAPTER 7

It was 1974 and I was living the good life. I had a fabulous apartment in New York and I had met Maria. Shaun had taught me how to drive and occasionally I would hire a car and take Maria for drives up the coast. I was investing in the stock market and putting many of the skills that I had learned over the past four years to great personal use. I was also learning to speak Italian. That is how I met with the beautiful Maria. Someone had left an invitation to 'Speaking Italian' on my desk, which was a cheese and wine night followed by an introduction to the courses available. I had mentioned to Olivia that I was frustrated at not being able to understand the 'Italian set' in the firm who often spoke in their native language, so after finding the invitation I decided to check it out. I went to the presentation night and subsequently enrolled for a course. I noticed Maria talking to various people and remember thinking it would be nice if she was one of the teachers. She was.

At first we didn't get along. I was struggling with the language and she was working me hard to keep up with the rest of the group. One time she embarrassed me in front of the class and I waited until everyone had gone home, before complaining. She quickly pointed out that I had expressly asked her to be hard on me, because I was keen to learn the basic language as soon as possible. She pulled me up during the class that night because I couldn't recite some fairly basic words. She put her face in mine and repeated the words over and over getting me to repeat them with her. Actually, she did this with all of the students in my class so I was just being paranoid.

One night, after our lesson had finished she suggested that I take some extra tutoring, which I thought was a good idea. "Tell you what," she said, "take me to dinner and we can talk about it." With that she grabbed her coat, closed up and we went and had dinner in a little restaurant near the language school. I told her my life story as I do with everyone I meet. I have always had this terrible habit of telling people everything about me since the day I was born. About all the characters I've come across, previous girlfriends and stories of my family. It's not a great idea to tell women about old girlfriends but I can't help myself. We finished our meal and I called a cab for her. I didn't want to blow my chances by suggesting I take her home or invite her back to my place, a real sign that I was finally growing up. Back in Ireland a date was considered a ride, clear and simple. The lads would only take a girl to the pictures, or a dance if they thought they were going to get somewhere afterwards.

I was several years into my apprenticeship, learning a second language and I had a kind of management role in the firm. As the weeks went by Maria and I became good friends and eventually lovers. I took Maria to a small island in the Bahamas called Bimini for a four-day holiday. That was the first holiday I'd taken since moving to the States. I felt a bit guilty at first because I knew that no-one in my family could go on a holiday like that. It seemed so extravagant yet it wasn't really expensive. The holiday was fabulous and the venue breathtaking. We wined, dined and danced every evening and spent the days swimming and lazing on the great beaches. We made love on a beach late one night under a stunning starry sky and I recall how I just couldn't believe my luck. "This is a long way from Farley Hill," I said to myself. This is something I would repeat all of my life when faced with moments or scenes of great beauty. Farley Hill was the housing estate where I grew up, and a place that seemed few could ever escape from. Maria had a wonderful time. We spoke little about her work or my business, which suited me fine. I had told her at the time of enrolling in the Italian course that I was an executive for a firm specializing in property development. She didn't seem that interested in what I did.

Maria Del Vecio never told me much about her private life, despite my giving her the top to tail version of my childhood on a daily basis. If I asked where she attended school, or suggested she recall some childhood memory, she would respond with one-liners. Maria was so pretty, I would ask, "why are you with me when you could have any man?" She would reply, "I could have any man but for now you will do." That annoyed me a bit. I was forever telling her how great she was and she just agreed with me.

I was always a bit self-conscious of my looks. American men were very healthy looking compared to me, and I was starting to become aware of this. I was wearing flashy suits to meetings and I wanted to be taken seriously. Image was important in the firm. If Gelli was making one of his rare appearances at the main office, the staff would drag out their best threads. Men who saw themselves as moving up in the organization spent a fortune on suits, Italian naturally. A good suit was the first step but you had to perform, deliver the goods. I knew I could deliver but I thought I could improve my image.

I started working out and often ran with Maria in Central Park. She was fitter than I was. It was like being in class again. She would run ahead yelling, "you must keep up if you want to get fit." It was worse than my school soccer training, although now I could afford proper runners. I didn't mind and I soon started to see results.

Although our relationship was gaining momentum we continued to live in our own apartments, which was important for me, because I often had visits from Gelli's people. These visits were never unannounced, unlike the early days with Shaun, but I couldn't be certain that this would always be the case. Gelli was such a high profile person that much of his and the firm's activities were monitored, by some Government department or otherwise interested party. In all the time I worked for Gelli I was never arrested on suspicion of anything despite many of his people being questioned over various crimes. The police would have known that I worked for, or at least knew Gelli, having seen me at many official functions run by the firm. These meetings were often under surveillance. Gelli had many friends in the police department. Some of these were very senior police. I helped make one of them, a certain police captain, very happy. I recovered some photographs which showed a young assistant playing with his baton.

His wife had hired a private detective to spy on her husband. She was planning a divorce. We trapped her in a sting. I called her and said that I was an associate of the private detective she'd hired. She couldn't confirm this with him because the good police captain had him in a cell on some bullshit charge. I told her that I was a lawyer who could get her a small fortune in settlement money and would she like to come to my office to discuss it. She agreed. I asked her to bring certain documents to the meeting.

We hired a serviced office and brought in the extras. I interviewed her and asked to see all the damning evidence she had on her husband, all the time reminding her of how much money I was going to win for her in court. She gave me the private eye's notes and the photographs, which I put with the negatives I had already recovered from his apartment. She was told that she would hear from me in a couple of days. I guess she would have eventually tired of waiting for my call and headed back to that office only to find someone else using the space. It must have been very confusing for her but I'm sure she would have figured it out eventually. After all her husband was a cop.

Maria was never to learn of my work, not from me anyway. We saw each other on a regular basis and the relationship certainly helped my Italian. In no time at all we could spend the entire weekend speaking only Italian. Gelli was very impressed with my new skill and on several occasions rang me speaking only in Italian the whole time.

Between 1975 and 1978 I worked on dozens of stings. In most cases I handled the complete operational planning. I barely saw Gelli through this period but was learning more about him and the Freemason group he belonged to. He was some kind of lodge leader. I had heard it referred to as P2. I never understood the full implications of this organization. Some of the men I had worked for were P2 members. They were quite open about their membership and bragged about Gelli's position. I'd never heard of these lodges in Ireland but I think they exist in most countries around the world. Apparently, freemasonry doesn't tell men what they are supposed to believe. Rather, the fraternity attracts men who already adhere to a set of beliefs about the nature of God, their relationship with him, and the moral conduct their God requires. The most important common ground of Freemasons is asserted before they become members of the fraternity, before they take part in any ceremony, before they take any oath. The application, or 'petition', signed by the candidate affirms that he believes in God and in the immortality of the soul. So, when anyone meets a Freemason, they can be certain that they are meeting a God-fearing man. Among the first words a new Freemason hears are, 'how you worship God is your own business, and how your Masonic brothers choose to worship God is their business and there will be no discussion of religion in the Masonic lodge. No Mason is to criticize any brothers' religious convictions or try to persuade him to change them.' Clearly then, every Freemason believes in freedom of religion.

In May 1978 Gelli, the Freemason introduced me to a man who was a former member of the Nazi party. This was the beginning of the end for me with Gelli and the firm.

CHAPTER 8

I had worked for a variety of people by now and I tried not to be judgmental because I was a crook, whichever way I looked at it. I used to console myself by saying that all the deeds I was doing were basically hoods settling scores with other hoods. In the main this was true. However, Arthur Rudolph was more than a mere hood.

During the Second World War, Rudolph was operations director of the Mittelwerk factory at the Dora-Nordhausen concentration camp, where 20,000 workers died from beatings, hangings, and starvation. Rudolph had been a member of the Nazi party since 1931. The 1945 US military file on him said simply: "Nazi, dangerous type, security threat, suggest internment." However, an American intelligence final dossier on him would say, "there is nothing in his records indicating that he was a war criminal, an ardent Nazi or otherwise objectionable." Rudolph became a US citizen and later designed the Saturn 5 rocket used in the Apollo moon landings. In 1980, his war record mysteriously appeared on the desk of a powerful DA, and Rudolph fled to South America. I did that job for free!

After WWII ended in 1945, victorious Russian and American intelligence teams began a treasure hunt throughout occupied Germany for military and scientific booty. They were looking for things like new rocket and aircraft designs, medicines, and electronics. But they were also hunting down the most precious spoils of all: the scientists whose work had nearly won the war for Germany. The engineers, and intelligence officers of the Nazi war machine.

The U.S. Military rounded up Nazi scientists and brought them to America. It had originally intended to debrief them and send them back to Germany. But when it realised the extent of the scientists' knowledge and expertise, the war department decided it would be a waste to send the scientists home. Following the discovery of flying discs and particle laser beam weaponry in German military bases, the war department decided that NASA and the CIA must control this technology and the Nazi engineers who had worked on it.

They had one problem: it was illegal. U.S. law explicitly prohibited Nazi officials from immigrating to America and as many as three-quarters of the scientists in question had been committed Nazis.

The US government saw to it that all records were destroyed. They did a good job considering how many men and how many records were involved but it was an almost impossible task. Gelli was still trying to retrieve damaging documents on behalf of these men, many of whom were friends of his, even as late as 1978 and possibly beyond. He told me that a dear friend of his was being accused of the most awful things by a group of people who were just 'German haters.' They were preparing to damage the credibility of a hard-working man who may have been involved in some unsavoury business during the war but was basically a good man. "They were times long passed," he reminded me. "We must help him." It was while stealing such a document that I learned about Arthur Rudolph. For this I had to travel to London.

There was a Jewish group in the UK putting evidence together to try and gain war crime convictions against a range of men including Rudolph. They would brag about the information they had and release excerpts to the press and journalists writing about the holocaust. I arrived at the group's headquarters in Tottenham saying that I was seeking information on this man for a journal I was writing for the Irish Times. They had no reason to suspect me of anything.

This was a job that almost didn't get done. After later reading stories that were so sickening, telling of inhumane treatment handed out by Rudolph on so many poor souls I was going to lie to Gelli and say that they had nothing by way of real evidence on Rudolph and leave it at that. I was actually going to return the documents I'd stolen but I didn't. However, I didn't destroy them either.

I had entered the group's office carrying a travel bag full of plain paper and various folders. I also had some marker pens and a label maker. I'd prepunched holes in the plain paper to allow me to make up a folder based on the size of any I might be shown. I had purchased the storage folders from a nearby office supply shop and they were the same as those used by the group. I simply asked the sales assistant in the shop if she could tell me which folders 'we' purchased last time and could I have some more. I assumed that someone from the office was buying stationary from the store and I was right! In fact, they had an account. The girl serving me was very helpful and even put the folders on their tab for me.

I told one of the staff what information I was looking for and he took me straight to the section which housed the file on Rudolph. He returned to his work leaving me to make up a fake folder, complete with nametag. I placed the original in my bag. I then asked the same guy if I could have a cup of tea. I put my bag near the main entrance and asked a man sitting at a nearby desk if it was ok to leave my bag there. He noted the bag and said it was fine. So now I would only be looking at the dud copy with its blank pages. I made a point of holding this up a few times so that anyone watching me would get used to seeing it.

After I had my tea I spent another ten minutes looking at the blank sheets and then walked back to where the folder had been stored. I carefully placed my fake copy back in the same slot saying out loud, "I'll put the file back here." The three men in the room were buried in files of their own and apart from a quick head glance from one of them they ignored me completely. I muttered that I couldn't remember where I'd left my overnight bag and reminded myself out loud that I'd left it near the entrance when I came in. In a moment I was gone and with me a file that may have taken these people ten years to put together. It is possible that they wouldn't have detected this theft for many weeks or months. It was in my London hotel room that I finally got to learn the truth about Lucio Gelli, the man I had worked for all these years. Right there, in the files I'd stolen, amongst all these murdering bastards was the man himself.

The document was a series of interviews; official notes from US intelligence and summaries by some members of the London based group trying to get convictions on people they claimed were guilty of war crimes. The notes on Rudolph were relatively short, because the available evidence was so damning. There was even a photograph of Rudolph standing next to a pile of bodies, with his colleagues, smiling for the camera.

There was one eyewitness account written by a woman who had been forced to watch as the Nazis slaughtered her family and left her alive to endure the pain. Her brother had stolen some item from Rudoph's factory, to sell on the black market. I stopped reading the reports at this point and lay down for a while to try and clear my head.

Lucio Gelli. I kept thinking of this man for whom I was working. How was it possible that he was associated with this group of maniacs? I couldn't believe that I had somehow become involved with a part of history that all decent men and women find abhorrent. My simple life in Dublin was looking pretty good now. Who was I kidding with this flashy go anywhere, own anything lifestyle. What of Maria? Lie after lie is all that she heard from me. I'd finally met someone I wanted to spend time with and I couldn't even tell her who I really was. I had started to deceive Maria the day we first went out together. She asked me what church I had been attending since arriving in New York. I told her it was Saint Joseph's. This was the church I walked past some mornings whilst out collecting the newspaper. I even went further to say that I always attended the 9 o'clock service. This made her happy. I doubted Maria had missed mass since she was a child. I hadn't been in a church since the police were after me, that day my childhood mates robbed a bank. I went to church to lay low for a few hours and save myself from the Garda.

I called Maria and told her I was finished with my business in London and that I would be flying back to New York the following evening. It was a brief conversation because she was on her way out to teach at the language school. I had forgotten about the time difference. She seemed happy to hear from me but I felt unsure. She didn't usually teach on Mondays. Maybe she had to fill in for another teacher. Why should I be questioning Maria, look what I had done for my day's work. I went back to reading the documents.

I had taken the entire folder, which had 'A class' written on the label and three surnames. Rudolph, Aps and Brennan. Aps, the report said was a paymaster in Hitler's Third Reich. Brennan was an executive with an emigrant savings bank in the US. It was while reading about Aps that I found Gelli's name under the heading, "known associates." The report on Gelli was longer than any single report on the three men under investigation: Gelli worked both sides. He helped to fund the Red Brigade, spied on Communist partisans and worked for the Nazis at the same time—a double agent. He helped establish the Rat Line, which assisted the flight of high-ranking Nazi officials from Europe to South America, with passports supplied by the Vatican and with the full acknowledgment of the United States intelligence community. The report continued; the U.S. participated in the war crime tribunals of key Nazi officials while maintaining an alliance with the Communist Soviet Union. Secretly, the U.S. was preparing for the Cold War and needed the help of Nazis in the eventual struggle the U.S. would have with the Soviet Union. Gelli's agreement with U.S. intelligence to spy on the Communists after the war was instrumental in saving his life. To understand Gelli the report said one must understand the complex post war years of Europe.

The biggest threat to Europe in pre-war times was Communism—it was the great fear of Communism that gave birth to the Fascists and the Nazis. Though both sides were dreaded, the Fascists represented right-wing government, while the Communists represented left-wing government. It was the right-wing that the United States and the Catholic church desired over communism—because communism would destroy the capitalist system. Prior to the second world war the CIA and the Vatican were involved in a joint venture, which provided support to the Nazis and fascists. The Vatican agreed to take part because they saw communism as a real threat to the church's survival. Italian communists would have taxed the church's vast holdings and the church has had a dismal experience with communist governments throughout the world—where religious freedom was stamped out.

I noticed that the author of the report was a priest from Rome. The Vatican appeared a number of times in the documents previously held by the British Government and this caused me to doubt some of the claims. Maybe it was all bullshit I thought. Coincidental relationships. Then, when I had turned to the back of the document folder I saw the final proof that Gelli had indeed been associated with at least the three men mentioned in these reports. There were a series of photographs inside a plastic sleeve with a small printed label marked, "surveillance." The relationships were not casual or coincidental. The London Boys may have been naive but they were thorough. They had photographs of all the men together and individually. One photograph in particular caught my attention. It was taken in the grounds of an impressive large house. Standing in a semi-circle with a group of seated ladies looking on, was Gelli, five prominent Nazi figures and a number of cardinals. The names of all attendees were hand-written on the rear of the well-preserved photograph. One of these cardinals would later be Pope. I re-read the documents closely, having skipped through the first time. There were more and more references to Gelli being involved with the Vatican.

The file included an abbreviated report on the Vatican, which spoke of Gelli having masterminded the distribution of Nazi treasure. The claim was that the Vatican had assisted in the storage and eventual sale of valuable items for the Nazi party. Gelli allegedly had made up an inventory of the valuables. They were broken down into categories and given valuations in US dollars. Gelli, according to the report, was acting as an auctioneer seeking bids from well-known collectors all over the world and in particular the United States of America. He was said to have flown these buyers or their associates to Rome to view the goods before purchasing, such was the commission Gelli could make. These viewings were said to have taken place at the Vatican itself.

The report included the names of Vatican officials who knowingly took part in the sale and distribution of the items and gave an indication as to the amounts of monies each of these men made. The amounts were staggering, even in today's terms. The report concluded by suggesting that the Vatican profited to the tune of one billion US dollars. I remember thinking, "this just can't be real." How could men who demand that the rest of us Catholics adhere to the teachings of Christ be such thieving bastards? I know that not all the priests and officials in Rome were a party to these activities but many must have been as the report indicated that there were thousands of items stored and eventually moved through Gelli's private Vatican warehouse. The Vatican was further accused in the notes about Brennan, of having full knowledge of the holocaust. It spoke of meetings between senior Nazi officials and Vatican leaders where the report says, compromises were sought. The Nazis were said to have given the Vatican assurances as to the timeline they were working on to solve the "Jewish problem." The Vatican treated its relationship with the Nazis as it would any other collaboration: documented, time lined, specific and filed.

The Tottenham boys had been playing with fire. They couldn't have had these facts for long or there would have been a massive exposé. Gelli and his friends must still have been working the relationships in Rome and the London group must have had a leak somewhere. I stayed over in London one extra day to allow me enough time to open a safety deposit box. That is where I left the documents. I flew back to New York and was debriefed by Gelli. It was over for me—just a matter of 'how do I get out?'

CHAPTER 9

❁

The first week back in New York I spent almost entirely with Maria, going to movies, nightclubs and restaurants. We went for walks in the park and made love every day. I was trying desperately to forget about London. If Gelli knew I hadn't destroyed the files I'd be a dead man. Rudolph by now was a very high profile man with NASA and the information I had would end that in a flash. I was thinking about moving back to Dublin. I thought Maria would love Ireland and I was sure my family would have loved her.

I had been back to Dublin just once and not for a holiday. I had a call from my eldest brother suggesting I fly home because mum was ill. He warned me at the airport that I might be shocked when I saw her. Nothing he told me could have prepared me for what I saw as we pulled up outside the house. My mother came out to greet me looking all of eighty or ninety years old. I was devastated to see her looking like this. She was only fifty-seven.

Despite her illness we had a good time together and I tried my best to act as though nothing had changed. I didn't brag about earning big money and I was careful not to say too much about my lifestyle. Dad and I had a few laughs but he could sense that things were not the same.

My older brother, who knew me better than anyone, asked me if things were going OK in America. He knew I would say yes even if I didn't have a pot to piss in. We have always been great competitors. There is a fair age difference between us two older boys and the two younger lads, thirteen years in fact. My elder brother and I were more like mates, whereas I never really had anything to do with the others. I guess I was a stranger to them, visiting mum that time. I regret now not spending time with them and with my three sisters. Family is all you ever really have.

Maria puzzled me. I was often away on business for weeks on end and yet she was always there, never showing any emotion one-way or the other. She really surprised me when she insisted that I go to Italy with her, and only just after I was thinking about taking her to meet my family. Her mother was not well and Maria, her only daughter, felt compelled to go and look after her for a while. She wanted to go straight away. She was a little homesick and missed her father. This was the first time that she had really spoken of her family. All of a sudden Maria had given me hope and an excuse to leave New York.

Maria had been sharing an apartment with another teacher from the language school, and like me, she didn't seem to have many possessions. Although I had my own place I didn't have much in the way of furniture and stuff. I went to see Gelli. He had been staying in New York to attend a farewell lunch for a major city official. I met him at his favourite club. I'd been there twice before as part of a group but this was my first solo gig. I wouldn't have gotten a job there, let alone be waited on as a guest, had it not been for Gelli.

The club didn't have a name, just steps that led to a big door and a big doorman. I knew my way to where Gelli was sitting enjoying his favorite drink, Turkish coffee, and soon joined him in swallowing something that Irish people used to repair roads. Normally I never spoke to Gelli until he said something first. The Club was quiet, like a library really. Gelli was relaxed and in between petite sips of tar acknowledged the occasional body that lurked in our part of this most private of men's clubs. I didn't wait; I just started mumbling something about a sick lady and Rome.

"Are you nervous?" Gelli asked.

"No sir!" I said, nervously.

"Relax and tell me your dilemma."

I took a deep breath, a swig of the God-awful coffee, and spluttered, "I need...ah...I've decided to go to Rome with my girlfriend Maria. Her mother is ill and I think I should accompany her...you know...give her my support."

I explained the whole situation to him with consummate awkwardness and plenty of repetition until Gelli stopped me. "Your friend sounds like a very responsible lady." He paused and wiped his mouth with one of his ever-present white handkerchiefs. "You are a loyal young man." He had said this very slowly and in a most threatening manner. I couldn't tell if he would kill me or wish me well.

Idiot I thought. You're not going anywhere. He didn't speak for over a minute, content instead to stare me out, which only took a second. I never have been able to stare people out save for one time with a young trainee counsellor.

Suddenly he puckered up his lips and said, "Go with her and look after your-self." He then gestured to the waiter to bring more coffee before leaning forward to pick up a beautiful leather briefcase, which bore the initials LG in bright gold lettering. He opened the briefcase and took from it a small package. "Before you leave I would like you to have this."

He handed me the package and told me that I was a trusted friend and he hoped I wouldn't be away too long. I removed the outer paper to reveal a small metal container. Inside I found a gold pin decorated with a crest of some kind. Gelli leaned over and took the pin from me before placing it into my jacket lapel. He then scooped the wrapping paper and metal container back into his briefcase. He sat down and voiced his approval at my new accessory, "That looks very smart." I thanked him, all the time being disappointed it wasn't some money to tide me over.

I told Gelli that I was sure we wouldn't be gone more than a few weeks and that I would get in touch with someone at the firm as soon as I returned to New York. No sooner had I finished saying these words, when a man appeared to show me out. I didn't look back and Gelli would not have bothered to watch me out, as a fresh pot of coffee was arriving.

I called Shaun who was now running a security business in Washington and asked him if I could store a few things at his place. I had already let my apartment go as I was due to move into a place I had bought a couple of years earlier. It was a house on the outskirts of the city. My tenants weren't extending their lease because the husband had been transferred to Columbus. I wasn't sure if Gelli had any involvement in Shaun's security business and I didn't care to ask.

Shaun and I hadn't stayed in touch all that much but we did remember to call each other on Saint Pat's and at Xmas. Shaun had also stayed at my place for a couple of nights about a year earlier, after a bit of a dust up with his girl. I owed Shaun for setting me up in the States but still couldn't help thinking, even as I spoke to him that time, that us two silly shaggers should go home and forget the whole thing. Noticeably missing from any of our conversations over the previous couple of years was Shaun's witty personality and I'm sure that he felt the same about me. He had also picked up the worst American accent.

My visa application only took a day or so to approve, thanks to a friend of Maria's who worked at the Italian consulate, so everything was sorted and we were off to Rome.

We arrived at the height of the tourist season. I took a room at a hotel near Maria's family home in Villa Borghese. Maria's family were devout Catholics and would have been disappointed with Maria if she had been living in sin. I didn't actually get to meet her family until around the beginning of the third week of my stay in Rome. Maria reported that her mother was getting better and then she let me know, quite casually, that she didn't want to go back to America. Somehow this didn't come as a surprise to me. When I arrived at Maria's apartment the day we were leaving New York, I found her standing on the front pavement partaking in what I could only describe as a long kiss good-bye to her flat mate. It was an emotional embrace for someone going away for a couple of weeks. I was also confused when I saw Maria's luggage, which was extensive, and I remember thinking at the time that her mother must be really sick with Maria prepared for a longish stay. Maria just said, "You can never have too many clothes" and I didn't take the luggage issue any further.

In response to Maria suggesting that she wanted to live in Italy, at least for a while anyway, I asked her if she wanted me to stay. She laughed, "Of course I want you to stay." She kissed me and told me that she was in love with me. She accepted my decision to stay without asking me about my job. Why would she think I could just walk away from a job like that? She had no knowledge of my earnings or if I could support myself and for how long.

I always had doubts about our relationship. We could make it together, but I would have to reveal some of my past to her. I asked the real estate people in New York to find new tenants for my house and called Shaun to say he could sell my things if they were in the way. I called the firm after I had been in Rome for a month and asked that Gelli be informed that I was planning to stay with Maria to see how things worked out.

"That's it," I thought. "You work for a rich and powerful hood and even knowing all the things you know you just leave, goodbye, adios amigo." Hardly, but I needed some fun in my life. I wanted to forget about Gelli, Rudolph, Sturgis, Peron and all the others like them, including me. Find the old me. Find that hopeless romantic that once fell in love with a girl who travelled only two stops on my local bus in Dublin. I like that kind of thing. You know how it is. You go to the shop for some bread and milk and the girl serving you is pretty. You stand there looking at her and just want to lean over the counter and give her a kiss. She just wants you to feck off so she can go back to talking with the other girls about their dates.

I rented a small townhouse near Maria's parents' place and became tourist for a while. My relationship with Maria was still fairly casual. It didn't seem to matter to her if we saw each other or not. When we were together she smiled and laughed and told me she was happy but at the same time if her mother needed her and we didn't see each other for a few days she didn't care. She never seemed jealous if I mentioned that I had met someone whilst travelling around the city and never gave me the impression she was waiting for a marriage proposal.

Maria and I enjoyed some great excursions during our first month in Rome. I loved that city. The ancient buildings, the artwork, the food, the people, it was all brilliant to me. The Colosseum was one of my favourite places despite its violent history. I could see myself sitting there in the great southern stand as a poor Christian came out to fight. I imagined the gladiator sticking his thumbs up to the lads in bay thirteen before relieving the scrawny Christian of his life.

Another great place was the Victor Emmanuel monument, (known locally as 'The Wedding Cake') not so much for the building itself but more for watching the traffic outside. The monument stands alongside a huge round-about. The road is wide enough but there are no markings and the drivers…well, they're Italian. Tourists love to watch the chaos at peak hour. Having a prang in Rome is as common as childbirth.

There were few attractions that I didn't visit, most times with Maria, but sometimes alone. I never joined the tour groups because they only spent a few minutes at each venue whereas I would spend a whole day. I admired these Romans who centuries earlier had built such fabulous and majestic buildings. I even found a pyramid in Rome, which contains the remains of a Roman magistrate.

I loved to see the artists displaying their work on the steps leading up to the Trinita' Dei Monti church. The skill of the local painters was awesome. Oil, pastel or water colour, it didn't matter, they were magnificent with any medium.

Maria and I both enjoyed the area around Villa Borghese and would often hire a rowing boat at the lake. Her parent's home was close by so we could walk the short distance to the lake or the zoological gardens, another favorite with both of us. There were times as we walked by the Tiber holding hands and sharing dreams that I really thought we were perfect together. Maria, however, had a habit of saying things like 'One day I will do this, or that' without considering me. One minute I felt secure and the next like I was seeing her for the last time. I thought she did things like that to make me jealous. I only had myself to blame for the way she treated me. I was so wrapped up in my work that Maria must have felt ignored or badly treated. But this was my chance to show her just how much I cared for her.

I surprised Maria with picnics, flowers her favourite pastries and even arranged for a local artist to paint her portrait. I took her shopping and bought her a collection of wacky hats that looked really stupid but made her happy. Maria loved hats and always wore a beanie. They made her look young yet sophisticated. Typical dress for Maria was dark jeans, polo neck sweater and a multi-coloured beanie. She wore dark lipstick and lots of mascara. Her eyebrows were plucked within an inch of their life and they framed stunning hazel eyes.

One day Maria asked me to take some photographs of her. She was planning to get one framed for her mum as a birthday present. We had a ball. The best photo was one with Maria standing in front of a tenement building which had all the washing strewn over the balconies. She took some of me which I hated, but it was only fair. We were just making our way to get them developed when we ran into a cousin of hers who was out jogging. Maria looked surprised to see him and I wondered if she was embarrassed to have him meet me. He was supposed to be some big wig in charge of the call centre for the main exchange in Rome. He bragged about how he was responsible for all the supervisors and telephone operators in greater Rome. I think I was impressed.

Maria hadn't introduced me to any family other than her mum and dad. Her father never said much to me but I got the impression he didn't have a great deal to say to anyone. Her mother gave her approval of me several times. The first time I met her I was very careful not to make a hash of it. I didn't use much of my Italian, as there is a real difference when you add the local accent. Slowly I introduced some Italian and she seemed impressed by this. "Do you love my daughter?" she asked, stern faced and right out of the blue. In Italy you simply didn't date a girl if there was no serious intent of marriage. "Cie, cie, of course I love her, of course." Her happy face returned and we were friends from then on. She would have had a heart attack if she'd seen us on the beach at Bimini.

So I was in Rome, my gal and me were becoming better acquainted and I was thinking of a business for myself. I was happy to stay there for as long as Maria wanted to. Little did I know how my life was about to change.

CHAPTER 10

It was mid September, I was relaxed, enjoying life and very comfortable in the old city. I had spent the day visiting various business people whom I was looking to recruit into a tourism venture. Basically I was trying to tie a group of hotels into a deal which guaranteed them a certain number of guests each night in return for some special pricing. I would take a few dozen rooms from each hotel, paying for them a month in advance. I would then offer a bribe to certain local booking agents, who worked for the international tour operators, in return for them selling my hotel rooms. The difference between the price at which the agent might sell the room and what I had to pay the hotel was my margin. It was all above board in an illegal kind of way. Europe's entire hospitality industry is controlled in one form or another by this type of networking with more backhands than a tennis tournament. The day had been successful with several individuals shaking hands over my proposal.

It was early evening and I was about to call Maria to see if she had eaten when there was a knock on the door. I didn't know anyone other than Maria so I assumed it was her. I opened the door to find two guys standing there. I couldn't make them out clearly, thinking they might be Mormons who were for ever chapping our door in Dublin. I flicked on the outside light and could now see they were priests.

"Buonasera gents…look, thanks guys but it's late and I was…"

"Per favore." One of the men cut me short.

"Look I…" Before I could say anything else they just pushed past me, walking right into my apartment. "What do you two think you're doing?" I asked, walking back in behind them. "I don't know who you are, now if you don't mind."

"Prego, si accomodi…prego!" The taller of the two men had told me to sit down.

I thought they could be armed, I was certain they weren't real priests. I did as he had asked and sat down. I was as nervous as hell.

"We want to hire you!"

I didn't respond.

"We want you to get something for us and we are willing to pay a great deal of money to encourage you to help us."

I thought I was dreaming. Here were two guys either lost on their way to a fancy dress party or real priests about to hire me to steal a consignment of rosary beads.

"Guys this isn't funny, have you got the right apartment?" I spoke in English all the while wondering what made them think I could understand a word they were saying. Now the other man broke his silence and in perfect English said, "We know who you are, and we are not in the wrong apartment. Perhaps we should give you some proof and then we can continue."

I sat frozen in my chair as your man rattled off with frightening accuracy details of my whole sorry life. Not just things I'd shared with close friends but the real dirt, as though someone had followed and recorded everything I'd ever done. No one could have repeated these things to me. It must be Gelli. Why? If he'd wanted me to do a job for him he'd come and see me or have someone contact me. But it couldn't be Gelli or they would have said so. My head was in a spin. Who? Who had given these two clowns my life story? Shaun, couldn't be Shaun, he wouldn't know the half of it. Maria had heard my life story often enough but then she knew nothing of my criminal history. There was a long pause without any of us speaking. I tried to visualize my time in the States in a matter of seconds, wondering which of the people I had worked for were behind this. Nothing made sense.

"Will you help us?" the shorter and much younger man asked.

I had to gain my composure and find out what it was they wanted me to do.

"There is a document, a package. We want you to steal it and bring it to us." "Where…where is the package?" I asked.

The man who had taken over as spokesman looked at his companion, as if seeking final approval before saying, "It is in the Vatican."

Oh thank God I thought, I am dreaming.

"The Holy City," he continued, "and we can assist you in gaining access to the area where the item is stored."

I had broken into banks, legal offices, private apartments, a police station, a judge's private home, but the Vatican? Jesus Christ, the Vatican!

"Let me tell you why we need to recover this document."

I listened to a story about a document held by some factional group leader inside the Vatican. The document supposedly contained information that, if leaked to the press, would be very damaging to the Catholic Church, and would severely undermine the credibility of the Holy Father himself. I was told that this man, who was in possession of the document had only one aim in life and that was to damage the long-term survival of the Roman Catholic Church. By now my guests had worked their way into chairs. The clothes they had on were tailor made, and they were immaculately turned out. Shoes with mirror like uppers and all creases razor sharp. The tall man looked more senior. If they were priests, I'd make him for a bishop at least. The younger man looked awkward and fidgety but nonetheless passionate when telling me how he believed their man was close to acting on his latest threat of making the information available to the world press.

What sort of information could be in such a document that might bring down the great Church of Rome? I remembered the references to the Vatican in the documents I stole in London. Maybe there was more to the Nazi connection. Maybe this renegade priest had the goods on the Vatican. The conversation continued. "We represent a group of priests who are dedicated to the one true faith. Many have donated all they have to help us gather together the money we know is necessary to employ someone…someone such as you. If this document proves that corruption exists, we will deal with it effectively, but in our own way. We have some knowledge of its contents but the press will focus only on the headlines and they will not investigate first, as we will do. None of us will condone any illegal activity by Church members past or present. But this is a matter of control."

Was this my chance at forgiveness? Help the mighty church and get absolution at the same time. Could it really be done? Could I actually break into the Vatican and steal a document? I reminded these guys that the Vatican was very well protected. However it was pointed out that the Swiss guards were only on the access gates and main entrance to the Vatican. Inside, the Vatican was responsible for all of its own security. I was told that I could be installed as a maintenance worker, which would give me access to the apartment where the document was housed.

These guys had lured me in. I don't know if I was bored or felt compelled to help but whatever it was I was now participating, making suggestions. "I'll need to know everything about the city. I'll need maps, copies of workers' schedules and details of the Vatican's day-to-day operations." I felt a rush. I rattled off more requests but before I could finish my guests stood.

"Grazie, We are grateful…the church will be grateful…we will be in touch." With this they left.

It was one of those unreal situations. I knew I would do it. I convinced myself that I had no choice. They would probably kill me if I didn't, having told me of their plans. If they were pretending to be priests, they had done a good job. They looked like priests. I don't know what bothered me the most, taking on the Vatican, or not knowing who I was working for. I had slipped back from relaxed tourist and budding entrepreneur to common thief in the blink of an eye.

CHAPTER 11

I stood outside the great church, completely overwhelmed with its construction. The Basilica of Saint Peter is massive and is the largest church in the world. The church can and often does hold thousands. Maria had taken great delight in telling me this. She had taken me there on our second day, firstly to pray for her mother and secondly to show me what a real church looked liked. She looked really proud as she showed me 'her' church. She knew the name of each chapel and a great deal about the history of the building, when each part was built, and who the Pontiff was during each stage of construction. The building is magnificent in every way and the Dome of St. Peters is simply awesome. Designed by Michelangelo it is the largest dome in the world measuring 42m in diameter and reaching 138 meters high. The interior, which includes 45 altars, is decorated by many of the world's most famous artists. Once inside you hear gasps of disbelief from many tourists; but the real sense of disbelief for me was the extravagance and utter decadence of the place. Would Jesus Christ ever have endorsed such use of resources?

The fresco painted by Michelangelo in the Sistine Chapel is the most popular attraction in the Vatican. The chapel itself looks quite ordinary from the outside and appears to have been attached as an afterthought to the main structure. Inside however, the great ceiling attracts millions of spectators. I saw people laying on the ground staring up at the great work and many art students making drawings of their own and taking notes. There were tour groups listening to expert commentary on the painting and others offering prayers at various points around the chapel.

The most stunning piece of artwork in the Vatican apart from the great fresco is a sculpture by Michelangelo called La Pieta. I looked at the face of the

Madonna holding the body of her beloved son Jesus and wondered how it were possible that something such as this could be carved by a man from stone. The expression on the marble face of Our Lady is more compelling than any painting or image that exists of her. It was even more magnificent seeing the work for the second time. Moments like that have always forced me to question my faith. I find myself moved in ways that can affect me for days on end. I know that they are just images and I tell myself that the stories of Jesus are just that, stories, yet I somehow find myself a convert. As a kid I would always make a joke when faced with these experiences. That was how I would stop myself from showing any emotion. I wish I hadn't made those jokes now. I used to think that men shouldn't cry but now I am scared of men who don't.

I had to remind myself why I was there again, surrounded by all this grandeur. My surveillance of the holy city had begun.

My new employers had provided me with maps of the interior. I'd also been given maintenance schedules and other information about security systems and guard stations within the city. I would not be able to walk the route of my eventual break-in as this was entirely out of reach for tourists. I would only see these areas for real on the day of the break-in.

Entry and exit points were my prime concern. I knew how I was going to gain access to the interior and I knew which part of the main building I would return to after I had stolen the package. All that was left was to determine the time it would take.

I watched the Swiss guards to see if they acknowledged any of the normal Vatican staff, but they didn't appear to. However, there did seem to be a lot of priests and other officials coming and going via the door that would be my initial passage and most of these people did acknowledge each other. My knowledge of Italian would be important here as there was always the potential for someone to strike up a conversation with me during the break-in. I had a number of things to check before the main event and I carried these out systematically. I checked and double-checked the things I could from the safety of the tourist area but now I had to plan for the break-in itself.

I'd been supplied with the official uniform of the Vatican City maintenance department. I had checked the fit and made a few alterations. I had an ID badge that I would wear around my neck and I had checked its authenticity against one of the workers at the Vatican. It looked identical. I checked my tools. I would only carry what I deemed absolutely necessary. I regarded myself as a specialist with locks but I had no idea what type of lock I would face once inside the target room. Jimmy Step taught me most of what I know but he used to say that ultimately you have to make it up on the day. There are hundreds of different types of locks and I had no idea what types I would find in Italy. I would take along a multifunction key that Jimmy had given me some years earlier and which I had used to open dozens of locks. It was a kind of good luck charm.

The one thing I wouldn't carry into the Vatican was a small charge that would normally accompany me. I would not damage anything inside this place. An explosive charge was only ever used to open safes that had welded themselves shut from age and long exposure to poor conditions. I had told Gelli during my first meeting with him that I would never rob a church. I convinced myself that this was different. I was doing the right thing by the holy church and I was adamant there would be no damage left behind.

Once again I would need to lie to Maria. I told her I was going to Florence for a few days to meet with some businessmen in relation to my tourist idea. All she could say was, 'have a nice trip and see you soon.' Would it be like this if were married? So casual. Sometimes I wished she would inquire more to see if I was cheating on her. Maria had told me that Florence was her favorite city outside of Rome, but she didn't even ask me if she could come along.

Everything was ready. The date was September 26th 1978. The following day I would take the documents from the holy city. I had a restless night, which was understandable. I lay in bed watching a replay of my whole life run before me. I couldn't help thinking how different my life would've been if I'd stayed home. What if I hadn't been expelled so early from school? Maybe if I'd stayed at the plastics factory I would have become the boss and seen more of Miriam. Most of the guys I grew up with married very young. This could have easily happened to me. I was deeply in love as a teenager and would have married at the drop of a hat. Truth is, I never considered it. I was wishing I had that night, as my stomach muscles squirmed around inside of me. Eventually I did get to sleep but even that was full of crazy dreams.

I saw myself living in the time of Caesar. I was dressed in a tablecloth while everyone else was dressed in fitted tunics. I was being hauled before some guy for stealing. My trial lasted about ten seconds because the man in charge had a busy day ahead of him. "Crucifixion," he announced and off I went with the rest of the local criminals to pick out my cross. It was the weirdest dream I'd ever had. Luckily I managed to sleep in for a bit that morning and I felt quite good when I finally got up. I had a solid breakfast, which I ate around noon before finalizing my plans.

I arrived at the Vatican mid-afternoon on the 27th. I was wearing the maintenance uniform and was carrying the tools I would require. I paused outside the main entrance for a few seconds, took a couple of deep breaths and moved towards the main doors leading to Saint Peter's Basilica. The guards on the main workers' entrance may have been regulars and show concern at not recognizing me. I had the correct papers to allow me safe entrance via any gate of the city but I wasn't taking any chances.

After following a group of tourists inside the great church I subsequently tacked onto another who were being led towards the Sistine Chapel. I was to move from the Sistine Chapel into the courtyard of the Sentinel through a tradesman door located at the rear of the chapel. This area, I had been informed, was lightly guarded most of the time. I paused for a moment under the great roof of Michelangelo where I was to gaze at the creation of the world for the third time. This gave me a sense of where I was and reminded me yet again that I was breaking one of my own rules about theft from places of worship.

As a kid in Dublin I once robbed a church with some mates of mine. We stole bibles, rosary beads, holy water bottles and the like. It was a meagre heist in the scheme of my life but it's the only time I ever felt guilty about stealing. Later in life I went back to the same church while on a visit home and placed a small fortune in the plate by way of saying sorry.

I located the rear door and there were no guards in attendance. I placed the master key I had been issued into the lock, unlocked the door and was soon through to the Sentinel courtyard on the other side. I closed the door and locked it again turning back to see that the courtyard I'd entered was empty. From here I moved into the Borgia Tower via an entrance door running off the side of the Sentinel courtyard and up a flight of stairs to the Borgia Apartments on the 2nd floor. There was a lone guard stationed at the entrance to the second floor and I didn't acknowledge him. I travelled along a narrow hallway, which housed a series of apartments and down a staircase into the enclosed courtyard known as the Triangle. I needed to use my key to open the doors, which lay at the foot of these stairs. When I opened the courtyard door I met with a young priest who was returning from the courtyard to the apartments. We didn't speak and he showed no surprise at my being there.

I continued on through a thin passageway that led off the eastern side of the courtyard and made my way into another small courtyard, which I recognized as the Sixtus V courtyard from the map I had studied. By now I had travelled almost a full circle but was heading towards the entrance believed to give me the safest access. The further into the holy grounds I moved the more nervous I was. What would be the penalty for breaking into such a place I wondered?

It had been agreed that I should attempt the break-in after 6pm, during mass, while many residents would be attending the various church services. I was ahead of schedule because I required decent light to make sure that I recognized the buildings, courtyards and doors necessary to gain entry. I entered a storeroom underneath a staircase rising up from the Sixtus V courtyard and decided to wait there until 6pm at which time I would move to the apartment area that housed the item I was to steal.

The storeroom itself was unremarkable, containing the usual cleaning apparatus and chemicals needed to maintain toilets, kitchens, carpets and the like. The staircase was old, possibly original. It was solid and supported by one large upright beam. Someone had carved their initials into the rich timber and for a manic second I was tempted to do the same.

At approximately 5.30pm I heard what sounded like marching and I realised that I was only a short distance from the Swiss Guard quarters. I reviewed the map in my head and checked that my torch and the other tools I had with me were in working order. A creaking noise, which came from the staircase, distracted me and without warning someone was unlocking the storeroom door. I quickly cowered under a workbench and pulled some sack material over me. I couldn't see who it was but assumed it was a security guard performing a routine check. My access pass and my well fitting uniform gave me the right to be there but what reason would I give for locking the door behind me. I could hardly come out from under the workbench and say that I was looking for something. If I was seen, I had a problem. I had never used violence against anyone to make good a break-in or an escape, and I wasn't sure what I would have done if I had been discovered.

I tried to stay as calm as possible. I played with the material and made a little peephole for myself. I could now see that there was a guard and he was making a thorough examination of the room checking that tools were in their correct places and that cabinets inside the room were properly closed or locked. There was some noise on the stairway again and this distraction allowed me to take a deep breath and adjust my position slightly. The security guard turned towards the door and I could see that he was looking out of the small window to see who had descended the stairs. He opened the storeroom door moved outside, closed and locked it again. I got my breath back and wondered if the noise on the stairs had disrupted the guard from pinching something.

It was now 6pm and quite dark. I left the storeroom pretending to check the door's hinges as I left, in case anyone was in the courtyard. I moved up the old wooden staircase, unlocked a double glass door and moved into a tiled entrance area, which led to a long hallway. On the inside wall there was a sign on a plaque that read 'Scala Nobile.' This was the area I'd been hoping to reach. The hallway contained several private dwellings all with similar looking entrances but clearly defined by different nameplates. I took these to be saints' names or special religious names written in Latin. This hallway looked like any entrance to apartments you might find in a city hotel or privately secured building. There were two sets of security personnel in this part of the building. The first pair was stationed at the midway point of the long hallway and the other pair at the far end of the hallway, which protected another staircase called the stairway of Pius IX.

By now I was not concerned with individual guards not recognizing me as these guards would assume I had entered by the normal workers' gate and would not see themselves as the first and only guards I'd encountered for the day. I didn't speak to the guards, pretending instead to be focusing on my Vatican notebook where, in Italian, I had written the words, "check and repair locks on windows to main room." I had done this in case anyone asked to see my maintenance notes, which I had been told where usually written down in the workers' notebooks to be signed off later, back at the maintenance control room.

I found the apartment I had been looking for at the end of the hallway. It was the last apartment and almost the last door. I could only see one small door further down. I thought that might have been an entrance to a storeroom or an emergency exit. The two guards stationed at this end of the hallway were on the other side of double glass doors at the top of the Pius IX stairway. The directions given to me had been perfect in every detail. I could now see the small grotto to the right hand side of the door, and a plaque with the word Excel was there just as it had been described.

CHAPTER 12

I opened the door using my maintenance key and found myself standing in another small entrance hall, lit by a miniature chandelier above me. There were two doors leading off this area. The door to my left was slightly ajar. I gently pushed the door back. I could see some bookshelves and a writing desk but apart from that there wasn't much else in the room. I pulled the door back to its original position before trying the knob of the second door. I had been told that the target room would be locked and that my maintenance key would be useless. Again the intelligence provided was correct. I studied the lock before opening a small tool bag, which contained my multifunction key along with some thin picks and a tension wrench. The multifunction key didn't work. I had never seen a lock like this one and would have to guess at how the locking pins were arranged. I inserted the tension wrench into the keyhole and turned it like you would a normal key. This turns the plug slightly off centre from the housing around it. While applying pressure on the plug I inserted one of the picks. I located the upper pins pushing each one into the housing in the same way that the correct key would have done. As each pin reached its correct position I could hear a slight click, which told me that the pin had fallen into place on the ledge in the shaft.

It was now more than 10 minutes since I'd left the main hallway. I hadn't planned on taking this long to work the lock. I quickly started work on the lower pins. Systematically I pushed each pin down until I heard the same click-ing sound. Finally the plug was clear and it rotated freely opening the door. I reset the lock, then quickly placed the tools back in the bag and wiped down the lock and doorknob. I entered the room, closed the door behind me, and turned on my torch.

A large table stood in the centre of the room surrounded by a dozen high backed chairs. Note pads sat neatly in front of all but the position nearest me. To the left there was a trolley with water jug and glasses and behind that an impressive ceramic pot atop an antique wooden stand. As I moved the light upwards I could see a large painting, which took up the entire wall space. It depicted the crucifixion of Jesus and was surrounded by a massive gold frame. As I swept the light to the other side of the room I saw a small altar. In the centre stood a tiny golden tabernacle with silver candelabra on each side. Across the top and down both sides of the altar I could see the raised timber paneling. I had been told that this concealed a safe.

I began to gently tap each section of the paneling listening for a hollow sound. There didn't appear to be a recess. I took out a pocketknife and ran it along each of the joints hoping to find a cap. The panel closest to the floor on the right hand side was not fixed along one edge and I was sure that this was a false door. I gently worked the knife into a space and pulled the panel back just a fraction. I checked that no cables were connected anywhere carrying power to a possible alarm system. There were none. I closed the panel and checked that there was no movement outside in the hallway. Everything was quiet. I prised the panel back open and inside found a small narrow alcove. Sitting on the middle of three shelves was a small wooden chest. The other shelves where empty and there were no other objects to be seen. I felt around at the back of the recess to see if there was a further panel or doorway because I'd been told that I was looking for a safe and so far every detail that had been relayed to me had been totally accurate. I couldn't see any possible hiding places so I decided the safe must actually be this chest.

The chest looked like a jewellery box with a reinforced metal strip around the edges. It was secured by one central lock. I picked the lock with ease and opened the chest. It contained only one small envelope. I held it up and shone my torch behind it. The envelope itself was almost see through and I could see that there was a small note inside. I couldn't make out the writing but was sure that this couldn't be the package I was after.

The back of the envelope contained a wax seal that had been broken. I slowly pulled back the top portion of the envelope and removed a small letter. Written on two short pieces of notepaper were about twenty lines of what looked like a normal letter or note but without a heading or sender address. The envelope itself contained no address, stamp, or attention to message. The note was unsigned and written in a language that I didn't recognize although I could make out the words Pope, Holy Father and a date. I was sure this couldn't be what they were paying me to steal.

I decided to see if there was anything resembling a damaging letter or document somewhere else in the room. I placed the envelope into a pocket in my uniform, closed the chest and returned it to the middle shelf in the alcove. I wiped the area thoroughly then closed the wooden panel over and pushed it in tight.

Just as I started to survey the room again I heard a noise coming from the hallway. I quickly walked towards a door at the far end and moved into what appeared to be a living room. I turned off my torch and took up a position that would allow me a narrow view back into the main room.

I heard the outer door close before seeing a shortish man enter the apartment turning on the main light. A second man had followed behind him placing some papers on the table before turning to leave. They didn't speak. I was trying to remain hidden while at the same time trying to see who the man was and what he was doing. He wore a priest or bishop's tunic and I thought he might have just taken mass in one of the Vatican chapels. Almost as soon as the first man had left there was a gentle knock on the apartment door. Two gentlemen wearing the clothes of church dignitaries not unlike the host had now entered the room.

One of the visitors told the man, whom I had yet to identify, that he was making a grave mistake. The second visitor agreed. They told him to reconsider his actions. The men had started speaking immediately upon entering the room without having been seated or without any formal greeting of any kind. I had to concentrate very hard to pick up on the exchange. "We really cannot agree with your decision, it will be damning" one of them said, but the short man, whose apartment I assumed I was in and whose private letter I had just stolen, told them both, "having met this woman I must tell you both how seriously I take her claims and how impressed by her I have become. I have decided to give the seer's warning full credence and I shall prepare myself to read the message given to us by the Blessed Virgin Mary, sometime soon. Regardless of its contents, I will make the information available to the public, as is the will of Our Lady. I have spoken out on this matter before today and it was common knowledge that once I had achieved my current position I would bring this matter to an end. I informed you of this several weeks ago and my resolve is firm."

The men didn't respond, just stood with heads bowed. The man hosting the two guests announced, "gentlemen, as Pope of Rome it is my solemn duty to fulfill these wishes of Our Lady of Fatima."

I was stunned. Had he just said Pope? I was in the apartment of the Holy Father Pope John Paul and I had just stolen from him. I couldn't understand this. It was well known that the Pope resided in the grand palace at the rear of the great church. These more humble, though not poorly dwellings were clearly the rooms of a lower ranked bishop or cardinal. Maria had told me that the Pope lives in a grand palatial apartment in the government palace. She was the perfect tour guide that day. She knew everything about the Vatican. She had worked there as a teenager preparing food in the kitchens of the palace.

"Your Eminence we implore you to reconsider." The visitors spoke in a strong, more purposeful tone. The Holy Father turned to the men and thanked them for visiting him but asked that they now leave. The two men looked at each other, turned and left the apartment without saying anything further, certainly anything that I could hear from the safety of my hideout. I heard the door close and the men were gone. The Holy Father had sat down and was now perusing the documents that had been left on the table.

I carefully closed my door and considered the options. The layout I'd been given hadn't included information about any rooms that lay beyond the main room. At first I thought I would hide until such time as I could make my way back to the main entrance but if these were the rooms of his Eminence the Pope I wanted to get out...quickly!

I could see three narrow strips of light on the far wall and assumed they were curtains so perhaps there would be a balcony. Though faint, the light helped me see objects in the room and other doors. I moved to my right and opened a door praying that its age-old timber wouldn't give me up. It creaked and pitched like a tethered ship and put my heart into overdrive. I turned on my torch to see that I had entered a large bedroom. My head was in a spin. The complex was like a labyrinth with rooms everywhere. A door stood either side of the bed with one more to my right. I moved towards this door thinking that I must now be parallel to the main room. I opened the door whilst at the same time taking the weight to reduce any pressure on the hinges. The room was a private library, narrow with both sidewalls stacked floor to ceiling with giant books. It had a small door at the rear with a safety bar to unlock it from the inside. This was the door I had seen earlier and had mistaken for a storeroom or general emergency exit. I closed the library door behind me and got ready to leave. I was concerned that the exit door would open very close to the guards at my end of the main hallway. They would have seen the visitors enter and subsequently leave and would have to question me if they saw me exiting via this door. Again, I considered the options. The balcony, if it existed was still an option as was hiding in the apartment until I could get back into the main room. Whilst I procrastinated about what to do, a flood of light washed under the library door. Someone was in the bedroom. The choice was made for me. I pushed the safety bar and the door gave way. Somehow I kept my composure and turned around to see the door close gently behind me. One of the guards on the other side of the glass hallway doors clocked me. I didn't know if he'd seen me come through the door or not. He lifted his head to acknowledge me but didn't move from his position and showed no interest in my activities. I took out my maintenance book, scribbled a couple of lines, pretended to check my watch and as I walked away scribbled a couple more.

I was able to leave the wing containing the private apartments with ease going back the way I had entered and then towards the Triangle Courtyard. Now I had to travel a different route because the Sistine Chapel would be closed and I didn't want to enter on my own in case cleaners or other 'real' maintenance workers were on duty. I had studied two possible routes out of the apartment building in case the theft had taken me past the official closing time for tourists. My heart was pounding. It's a wonder I didn't just leg it through the nearest gate.

With all the confusion going on in my head I somehow managed to remember every step of the second escape route. My new route saw me move from the Triangle Courtyard via a small door on the western side into the Inscription Gallery, down a small outside lane-way and through the Apostolic Library where many priests were studying. A student priest stopped me in the library. I nearly choked. He was seated at one of the many desks provided, but the reading light at his station wasn't working properly. He waved his hand to attract my attention without disturbing the other readers. At first I thought I would ignore him but a number of priests using the facility had noticed me and could see that the man was trying to get my attention.

I walked over to him trying to act as normal as possible. I was clearly out of breath and my mouth was so dry I feared I wouldn't be able to utter a single word. He pointed to the reading lamp and I nodded. He continued trying to read by what little light he was getting from the two roof lights and I wandered off to see if I could find a maintenance cupboard in the library.

I went into the staff room near the library entrance, walking in on two men playing cards. They were both young, about twenty, and without introducing myself I told them to go and check the reading lamps, as some of them were faulty. They immediately stood up, apologizing profusely for not knowing of the faults and left the room. I stood with my back against the wall and composed myself. There was a large mirror over a sink on the wall opposite and I saw a scared man looking out at me. I couldn't believe that they didn't wonder who I was, just barging in like that.

I didn't stay in the room long in case the two men returned to involve me in a conversation. Though my Italian was good I didn't have a great knowledge of local issues like soccer results, something that could have brought me undone. I opened the door slightly and could see the two genuine maintenance workers checking all the reading lamps. I left the staff room and approached the staircase near the entrance. I moved up to the second floor into the gallery of maps and then down the rear exit to an area I knew as Stradone Del Glardini. From there I moved along a roadway towards St. Peters, past the fountain of the Sacraments and across a landscaped garden just north of the great Church.

I entered the Basilica through a maintenance door almost bowling over a cleaner. I told her I was sorry and helped pick up the items I'd made her drop. I felt strangely at ease as I made my way into the church and sat down to contemplate what I had done. I should have bolted straight out of there but told myself I hadn't stolen anything. I even thought about posting the man back his letter. There was no package, no documents. Perhaps I had the wrong room. I tried to relax my breathing. Look as though you're praying, I said to myself.

I opened the envelope again, being careful not to damage it in any way. I stared at the words on the page for the second time and wondered what could be so important. The name of Pope John XXIII was there but apart from this and the words Holy Father I could understand nothing. The handwriting was beautiful, almost print quality, with perfect rounded swirls on certain letters. Again, I noticed there was no heading, no sender address and it was not signed or initialed. There was a date at the end of the second line: August 20, 1959. I think the word was August, it looked to have been misspelled but the numbers where clear.

I looked around the great Church and I was almost alone. I could hear footsteps to one side but there were clearly few people inside the building. I needed to leave. I stood up and walked to the end of the pew and stopped in the aisle. I looked at the altar but didn't bow. I just turned my back and walked straight out. There was nobody attending the doors. I walked down the stairway, marched across the car park and beyond, to the residential street where I'd left my car. As I got closer to my car the walk became a jog.

CHAPTER 13

I drove over the river to Villa Borghese. I knew my way around there. Maria and I had walked there so many times. I parked the car in a secluded part of the gardens and just lay back in the seat for a minute. I was damned if I could make sense of it all. Gelli...Lucio Gelli must be behind this. I held the envelope up in front of my face and told myself that I was clearly missing something. Whatever it was the men wanted it was here, here in this sweet little note. I stared at it for ages, all the time looking around to see if anyone had followed me.

I was meant to take the package to a place on the other side of the city. I knew I couldn't hand it over. I'd been deceived enough; no mention was ever made of the Pope. Who has the right to steal from the Pope? Certainly not my employers. I didn't even know who they were, and definitely not me. Suddenly amidst all the crazy thoughts and wild speculation, the words of the Pope came to me: "Gentlemen, as Pope of Rome it is my solemn duty to fulfill these wishes of Our Lady of Fatima. Regardless of its contents, I will make the information available to the public, as is the will of Our Lady. I have decided to give the seers' warning full credence and I shall prepare myself to read the message given to us by the Blessed Virgin Mary, sometime soon."

Fatima, I knew this name Fatima. When I was a child we learned of a girl from Fatima in Portugal who had seen Jesus or God or the Virgin Mary or all of them. I couldn't remember, but I remembered the story. She wrote a letter or a message telling the people of the world about a secret from God or Jesus. I think it was about the end of the world. The message was to be read out on some day or at some particular time. Is this what I had? The letter from the little girl? That would be special and it would be hidden in a safe place. But what possible value was it to the men who hired me? Maybe it was stolen for a collector? Perhaps it had some value among people who wanted to own pieces of history. I couldn't hand it over without knowing what it was.

My strongest urge was to return it to its rightful owner. The men who hired me would know by now that I wasn't coming. They would certainly be looking for me. I couldn't go back to my place. I should call Maria. How could I ever explain this to her? She would almost certainly know the story of Fatima but what would she make of my inquiring after such a tale. I had told her I was in Florence, how could I change that? I needed to rest and get some food. I drove into the city and stayed the night in one of the smaller hotels. I was so dazed that I wouldn't have noticed if I had been followed up to the hotel room. I sat on the end of the bed, head in hands, pushed myself back and sprawled out on the bed looking up at the ceiling. Not quite the Sistine Chapel. The paintwork here was about to fall off. The room smelt of cigarettes. I didn't smoke but the smell made me want one. If I could just sleep it off!

I woke up about 9.30am after the best sleep. My room had an excuse for an en-suite so I got up and had a hot shower. After the shower I laid back down on the bed, suddenly feeling exhausted again and now thinking about the Fatima story. I dressed and decided to visit some bookshops or a library to get what information I could about the events in Fatima. I walked into a busy shopping area where the tourists were buying their keepsakes. I found a large bookstore and went in. It wasn't hard to find the religious section, which took up half the store. I searched the titles for a minute before finding a whole series of books about Fatima. I preferred an English version and eventually found one.

The story of Fatima. I browsed through and could see from the headings that it would have all the information I was after. I was just about to turn away when an assistant spoke to me.

"She's still alive you know."

"Excuse me!"

"The lady," she continued, "she is still alive."

I told the assistant that I was interested in the story and asked her if this was the best book available. She said it was the best English version she had. She also told me that one of the three children who had allegedly seen The Blessed Virgin Mary at Fatima was still alive and living in Spain or Portugal. She was a Carmelite nun. I thanked her for telling me what she knew about the story, bought the book and returned to my hotel.

I read it from top to bottom, every word. It was a coffee table book with large pictures and maps of Fatima and Portugal. I read about the secret message. The book claimed that one of the seers, as they were referred to had written down the last part of a message given to them by Our Lady who wanted the message revealed to the public before 1960. This may have happened. I needed more information. The book was vague, more like a tourist version and I needed a history book. I went back into the city to see if I could find a library somewhere. Instead, I went into another bookstore that appeared to be an educational store with textbooks and encyclopedias. I told one of the assistants that I wanted a book about Fatima that included eyewitness reports or newspaper articles. The man who served me knew exactly where to look. I ended up buying two more books and returned to my hotel stopping only to get something to eat and drink in preparation for a great deal of reading. I read for hours. Making notes. Checking one books stories against another. Checking one eyewitness account with another eyewitness account. By late evening I was very tired. I was thinking of calling Maria but it was late and my head was not clear. I told myself I would call her first thing tomorrow.

I awoke the next morning feeling very thirsty so I dressed and walked to a corner store to get something to drink and maybe some breakfast. There were people standing outside the store, deep in conversation and looking very animated. I went into the store and walked over to the drink section. I picked up a carton of orange juice and walked over to the counter. On the counter was a stack of newspapers. The headlines read, "Pope Dead."

"The Catholic Church is in mourning today after the death of Pope John Paul I RIP." I bought a copy and raced back to my hotel. I ran up the stairs and hurried into my room where I spread the paper out across the bed. The main stories were about the life of Albino Luciani the quiet Italian who became Pope little over a month earlier. Then I saw it. A reporter had written, "though Vatican officials have decided not to release the details of the Pope's death, I can confirm that there are reports of a man being seen entering the Vatican City on the afternoon of the 27th. Speculation is that this man may have lay in wait for twenty four hours in a plot to kill the Holy Father."

I'd been set up. The official Vatican press releases didn't mention anything suspicious but I also couldn't find any mention of an illness or an accident. The Vatican hadn't said anything really. The Pope, dead at 65. The whole thing was a fit-up from the start. The report about a man seen at the Vatican was buried in the paper. It was part of a series of one-liners. Perhaps it was just the early onset of conspiracy theories. On day one? I was drawing a long bow.

They'd hired me to steal this piece of nothing in an envelope and no doubt had me followed. There would be photographs eventually. They would build a case. I had to leave Rome immediately. I couldn't trust going back to my apartment. I decided to call Maria. There was a call box in the hallway on the ground floor. I called her up. Her mother answered and she sounded distraught. She didn't say anything past hello and kept sobbing but she got Maria for me.

"Where are you?"

There was some urgency in her voice that I had never heard before.

"Where are you, are you nearby."

I went to speak but hung up the phone instead.

I packed up all the books I had bought and folded up the newspaper. I went straight to my car and decided to go north. I drove for only a few minutes when I stopped the car. I realised that if I went away I would never be able to get my things from the apartment. I had almost no money with me, no passport and all my bank details were in the apartment. I had to get them. I could enter from the rear of the building. I convinced myself I could tell if anyone was watching the place. It wasn't far to drive and I would rush in and out as quickly as possible.

I parked in the area at the rear of the small apartment building and everything looked calm. There were some people talking across rear balconies but given the day's headlines, this was to be expected. I didn't speak to anyone. I went in, grabbed money, personal effects, poured some clothes into a suitcase and was gone in what seemed less than a minute. I headed north out of the city. I role-played every scenario on the drive and when I became tired I invented new ones. I drove for several hours only stopping to eat, go to the gents or buy a late edition paper. Finally I pulled into a motel and crashed out. I slept for a few hours had a shower and then did some exercises to try and relax.

Every theory possible was now filling the papers. The Vatican had still not released any official cause of death. More reports of a man seen entering various parts of the internal complex. Only the men who hired me knew that I had been in the courtyards mentioned. I had been spotted by a couple of people but the reporter was suggesting sightings that were only guesswork, perfectly accurate guesswork because he had been fed this information. There were no official police reports and there was no suggestion that they were looking for anyone. One lone reporter was getting his piece across, always buried in amongst general pages. This same reporter had compiled this tribute to Albino Luciani with comments from friends, family and fellow priests.

Albino Luciani had been a popular choice for Pope having been elected on the first day of the conclave by an overwhelming majority. He was considered by many in Rome as 'God's candidate' for Pope. He immediately dispensed with some of the formalities of the papal office and was inaugurated with the investiture of the Pallium rather than being crowned with the traditional Tiara. The article reported that this had raised more than a few eyebrows in the Vatican, particularly amongst the elder statesmen. Albino had collaborated closely with Pope Paul VI, the man he succeeded and had indicated abhorrence to the suspected corruption prevailing inside the Vatican. Albino Luciani's career was punctuated with political comments such as the one he made in Venice when he suggested that all parish priests sell their church ornaments and jewels for the benefit of the poor. I imagine that went down like a lead balloon much as another comment would have when he suggested that the Catholic Church donate 1% of its annual income to support poor churches in the third world. His death, after just thirty-three days in office, marked the shortest reign in the papal office since that of Leo XI in 1605, which had lasted just twenty-six days.

There was an interesting footnote from a fellow priest who said that on July 7th 1935, the day that he and Albino Luciani were ordained, he remembers the brash young priest rejecting a gift from a well wisher saying that the church must reject all material wealth. The gift was a gold rosary set, which Albino said could feed a family for a year. The priest being quoted said that Albino commented that the church would one day be chastised for its obsession for material wealth.

I put the paper away and returned to the Fatima books. Was there really a connection? I read for the rest of the day learning everything about the children from Portugal and tried desperately to see if any clue of what might connect these events would present itself. It didn't. There was no one thing that could possibly tie these two events together.

In 1917 Lucia Dos Santos aged 10, while accompanied by Francisco Marto aged 9 and Jacinta Marto aged 7, was looking after a herd of sheep in a field near Fatima Portugal, when the Blessed Virgin Mary appeared to the children. Between May 13th and October 13th of that same year the Blessed Virgin Mary, appeared six times to these three children. The Blessed Virgin told them that she had been sent by God with a message for every man, woman and child living in our century. The heart of Our Lady's message to the world is referred to as the 'secret', which she confided to the three child seers in July 1917. The secret actually consisted of three parts, the first two parts having been publicly revealed. The book then went on to say that the last part of the secret has not yet been made public but was contained in a letter written in January 1944. I went on to read that Lucia, now called Sister Lucy had recorded the message on notepaper whilst living in a place called Tuy, in 1944. The message, it said was to be made available to the public on her death or before 1960, which ever occurred first. She claims that Our Lady only revealed this final part of the message to her.

The book went on to speculate what this note could contain but admitted to the fact that no one really knew the answer, no one other than Lucia and perhaps one or two Popes, who are rumoured to have read the secret message. The books were written a while ago; maybe she was dead by now. The girl in the bookshop did say she was still alive. I decided that the only person who might help me unravel this mess was the author of the letter I stole from the Pope, the man who someone was accusing me of murdering.

CHAPTER 14

The newspaper tributes continued for days and still the Vatican had not given any indication as to the cause of death. The reporter who had first mentioned a possible link with a supposed intruder was continuing his lone crusade. His latest revelation was the suggestion that an unusual item had been located by a cleaner and was being examined by police. I couldn't imagine what that could be as there was no way I had left anything at the scene. His stories were still not making any headlines but someone was giving him space in the paper each day to make his claims. Still there was no mention of a police investigation.

I had to find Sister Lucy. I couldn't just go on a sojourn to Portugal or Spain on the off chance that I might locate her. I had to be sure she was alive, know where she was and pray that she would see me. The books that I'd read gave some indication as to where she might be living. I had read details about her life after the apparitions. A forward in one of the books pointed out that Sister Lucy had devoted her entire life to her chosen faith after having been introduced to the Dorothean Sisters as early as 1921. It was there in the mid-twenties, after moving to Tuy, that she took the habit with the name Mary Lucy of Sorrow, with her final solemn vows coming in 1934. She moved to Coimbra in 1948 joining the Carmel of Saint Teresa, taking the name of Sister Mary Lucy of the Immaculate Heart. That was 30 years earlier; it would be a fluke if she were still there.

I thought of just calling the convent. What would I say? I couldn't speak any Spanish or Portuguese so how would we communicate? Maybe the Carmelite nuns didn't speak at all. I had two aunts who were nuns and you couldn't stop them from talking. My older brother and I ran riot in their convent in Belfast during one summer holiday. I also attended a school run by nuns, the Little

Sisters of Mercy. They went by various other names from children who were schooled under their regime of terror. As for Little Sisters, they averaged about 90 Kilos apiece!

This was at a time when nuns were nuns, mean, nasty, and vicious, with good aim. In second grade I met with one particular terrorist called Sister Rita. She was our teacher. She looked to be in her mid-twenties, really old to us nippers. She, like all the other nuns came dressed in the common uniform of the day, black robes. The robes had very deep pockets able to conceal chalkboard erasers or other dangerous projectiles. All had their Rosary Beads looped around their waist dangling on their right side. All wore black shoes and stocking or socks. And of course they all had that same hat. It was called a 'habit' and it looked like a black flat hat that covered the entire head with a white collar wrapping around the forehead. A veil topped off the look and covered all the nuns' hair. Hell, you couldn't even see their ears. But let me tell you, they could hear better than dogs. Dare to talk in class and be prepared to absorb the wrath of Sister Rita. Usually, she would spin and fire an eraser at your head. Nine out of ten times, it would connect. The one time it missed you, it would smack an unsuspecting innocent kid sitting next to you. Those were the only times I ever saw Sister Rita smiling.

As that school year progressed, I started to become obsessed with the secrets that lay beneath the nun's habit. Was there another pair of eyes under there? A listening device of some sort? More erasers? I began to devise a plan to unlock the secrets and remove the habit from the nun. As we were coming in from recess one day, I got in behind Sister Rita and followed her until we almost reached our room. Then, I did it. With one swift fast motion, I grabbed the back of her habit at the base and yanked as hard as I could. I awaited the treasures. Instead, I was shocked to see that instead of removing the habit, I had actually pulled Sister Rita off her feet and flat down on her back. Little did this seven year old realize that the habits were attached to the nuns head by an intricate pattern of bobby pins and hair clips. Hurricane winds would not have removed that habit. On the bus ride home that day, all the buzz was about me and how I had knocked a nun down and dragged her through the halls and all that. Even the bigger kids came over to get a good look at me. For about a week, I was a celebrity, one to be reckoned with, one to stay out of his way, that was until one day when another kid got stung by a hundred or so bees that he'd been bothering with a stick. I passed the torch to Declan, the bee-keeper.

I had no other option but to simply telephone the convent and hope that I'd get somewhere. I used a street phone because the only phone in the motel was in reception and offered no privacy. I asked the operator to connect me to the convent of Coimbra, Portugal. She asked me to repeat the request and I did. There was a pause then a second person came to the phone, a male.

"Hello, I speak English sir, you wish to speak to a convent in Coimbra yes?"

"Yes please."

"Which convent sir, there are more than one."

I told the operator it was the convent of the Carmelite nuns.

"Certainly sir, if you can be patient I will try to connect you."

The operator was very efficient coming back to me and telling me the line would soon be available but I was feeling anxious and trying to hurry him up.

"There you go sir, you are connected."

I was through and the line was good. The woman who answered the phone didn't seem to understand Italian or English. I asked if she knew of a Sister Lucy as I was trying to contact her. I repeated the name Sister Lucy several times. There was no reply and I thought the phone had gone dead. I waited ages occasionally saying, "hello…hello," still no reply. I was about to hang up and try calling again when a second lady came to the phone who spoke Italian perfectly.

"I understand you wish to speak to Sister Lucy, do you mean Sister Mary Lucy?"

I said I did and apologized for not giving her full name.

"What is your business?"

She was very blunt. I thought they mustn't get many personal calls, or maybe because of her history Sister Lucy gets hundreds of calls. I knew that if this was the right convent and Sister Lucy was there I only had one chance of speaking to her. I must mention the envelope.

I told the woman on the phone that my business was to return something to the good Sister. Something she would like returned, very much.

"What is it, can I know?" the woman asked.

"Please tell Sister Mary Lucy that I have a small package containing some papers belonging to her and I would like to know if I may return it in person. Can you tell her that it is the package from Tuy, with the red wax seal on the back." The woman asked me to wait and as I did I pushed what few coins I had left into the phone hoping they would last. I waited for a couple of minutes before a new voice came on the phone.

"Hello senor, you wanted to speak?" a lady spoke in slow broken English.

The operator came back on the line. "One minute you have one more minute for the connection."

"Sister…is that Lucia, can we meet please." I must have sounded like I was pleading with her.

"I go stay a convent at Tuy in tomorrow. Are you in Portugal senor?"

I told her I could meet her in Tuy not mentioning the fact that I was currently in Italy. She told me it was the convent of the Dorothean Sisters near the centre of Tuy. Just as we agreed that Friday afternoon would be the time for our meeting, the phone line dropped out.

I felt some degree of success for having made contact at least. I hoped that Tuy would be easy to get to. I didn't know anything of Portugal or where Tuy was.

Tuy was actually in Spain; bound on the north by Pontevedra, to the east was Orense with the Atlantic Ocean to its west and Portugal to the south. The liner notes in one the books I'd bought said that the city, which has a population of 3000, comprises the civil provinces of Orense and Pontevedra and is very ancient. I remembered that it was whilst living in Tuy and probably in the same convent that Sister Lucy had written down the message, which I believed I was carrying.

One of the books I'd purchased had a full chapter on the events that led to the message being committed to paper. Sister Lucy was worried that if she fell ill and died the secret part of the message, revealed to the children would be lost. The claim was that when Our Lady spoke about the final part of the message she told Lucia that she was only speaking to her now. The other two children had heard most of the message but were not allowed to hear the final part or 'warning' as the books author(s) all agreed it must be. I read about the other two children who witnessed the apparitions along with Lucia.

Francisco Marto was born on June 11, 1908 he was the Son of Manuel Pedro Marto and Olimpia de Jesus Dos Santos, modest farmers and good Christians. He died on April 4, 1919 of the epidemic called 'Spanish influenza'. I read that from the time the young seer met with the Virgin Mary, Francisco developed a total disregard for earthly goods and for his own life and health, spending the days in ardent expectation of entering heaven. After his death his parents revealed that Our Lady had informed Francisco that his life would be brief. His mother said of him that he was truly the living faith. The story I was reading included many eyewitness accounts and included confirmations from Lucia herself about their accuracy. I continued reading. Lucia asked Francisco shortly before his death if he was in pain to which he replied, "quite a lot, but never mind. I am suffering to console our Lord and afterwards and within a short time, I am going to heaven." He said the rosary every day and countless locals visited to pray with him. The book was filled with photographs of the children and the area around Fatima where the children claimed to have seen the beautiful woman, as Jacinta called her.

Jacinta Marto was born March 11, 1910. Younger sister to Francisco, she was also to die of the same killer influenza on February 20, 1920. It is said that she was constantly immersed in the contemplation of God, in intimate colloquy with him. She sought silence and solitude and at night she got out of bed to pray and freely express her love of Our Lord. In a little while, her interior life became distinguished by a great faith and by enormous charity. Unlike her brother, Jacinta died alone in a Lisbon hospital far from her loving parents and acquaintances. She had been a patient at the hospital for some time. On the day of her death she had requested the sacraments but only received the sacrament of Penance. Conscious of being near death she requested Holy Viaticum, but the priest not withstanding the pleas, deferred it to the following day. He never explained why he chose to do this. She had finally reached the goal of her desires, eternal life. At the same time that she confided the Fatima Secret to the three seers, the Blessed Virgin also promised that God would work a great miracle the following October, "so that all may believe."

I had become fascinated with the whole story. I couldn't help thinking how my Dad would feel if he knew that I was somehow involved with one of the great religious stories of the 20th Century. I had heard him mention the Fatima story but I never took much notice of it. I guess I would have dismissed it as nonsense. These children saw something in the fields at Fatima. I don't know what it was but it was enough to make Lucia devote her life to God.

I needed to plan my trip. At first I thought of driving to Tuy but a quick look at a map made me realize that it was at least a thousand miles from where I was. I decided to drive back to Rome instead and fly from there to Portugal. I would then hire a car and drive north to Tuy. Having an Irish passport was a bonus. Even at the height of the 'troubles' in Ireland our passport would get you a visa to visit any country with few questions asked. I didn't go back to my apartment in Rome, instead spending the night near the airport. It had taken me less than an hour to get the necessary visa documents in the city and I was able to book a flight for the next day to Lisbon. I could have also booked a connecting flight to a city close to the border but I decided to drive from Lisbon through Fatima and finally on to Tuy, Spain.

Despite the continuing story in the press about a mystery man seen wandering around the Vatican I was convinced that the police were not looking for me. The story was for my benefit only. Warning me to return the envelope to the men who had hired me. I wasn't scared to take a flight, as I didn't think that the police would be waiting for me at Rome's airport. I still had no idea as to who had hired me. Was it just a set up to implicate me in the Pope's murder? Was he murdered? I desperately wanted to speak with Maria. I couldn't call her. I needed to have this sorted out. When it's all finished I told myself, I'll call her then.

It had been five days since the first reports of the Pope's death. I was buying morning and afternoon papers to keep abreast of the story. The morning I was to leave for Lisbon the rogue reporter's stories had taken a giant leap forward. Front-page news.

> 'Local authorities are now taking seriously claims that a man was seen entering the Vatican late on the afternoon of September 27th. It is believed the man was wearing standard issue maintenance uniform, which he had stolen from the home of a Vatican laborer. He is described as being 172cm tall, black hair, skinny build and is said to have an Irish accent. He apparently spoke with several people whilst moving through the interior of the Vatican City disguised as a maintenance worker. It is believed the man was responsible for a theft from the apartment of the Holy Father.'

The report also said that Vatican officials have denied there were any signs of a break-in or burglary. There was still no official word as to the death of the Pontiff. I expected to see my picture in the next edition.

I really couldn't believe that all this was for the little note written by Sister Lucy. Clearly the men behind this thought I had stolen some fantastic document with a devastating expose of fraud and corruption. What if I just handed it over to them? Show them that all I took was a harmless little letter. It was too late. I'd had too much time to conjure up any number of wild stories. These men knew of my expertise in stealing and handling documents. They would only believe I had 'whatever' they had sent me to retrieve. The timing of my flight couldn't have been better.

CHAPTER 15

There were no police guarding the airport as I left Rome that day. I was looking at everyone, suspecting everyone. If the police were following me they would never have let me board the plane, I was sure of that. The flight was good apart from some minor turbulence as we approached Lisbon. The plane was packed and I learned that I was lucky to get a seat at such short notice. It was peak tourist season for Catholics on their way to Fatima to celebrate the events of 1917.

I sat next to a priest who informed me that a great miracle was performed in Fatima on October 13th 1917 and that thousands of people from Italy and many other countries visited Fatima around this time each year to celebrate this wonderful occasion. He was taking a group of sick children with him in the hope that another miracle may take place. He said many people had claimed to be cured of sickness after visiting Fatima and praying in the fields where the Blessed Virgin Mary appeared to three children. I had read about a miracle in the books I had purchased. Maybe this is why Sister Lucy was going north to Tuy. It would be common knowledge to those who had followed her life that she resided in Coimbra, near Fatima. I wondered if her decision to travel at this time was to avoid a possible demonstration of affection for the Sister causing massive disruption to the people of Coimbra and the convent there. The priest gave me a booklet to read, which was part of a tourist guide to the religious events in Fatima.

During the last apparition, on October 13, 1917, the lady of light revealed herself to be our Lady of the Rosary. 70,000 pilgrims, rain-soaked from earlier showers, were waiting with the seers to witness Mary's final appearance when they saw the sun spin out of its orbit, emitting a rainbow of colour as it gyrated. Finally, when this display ceased, the sun was seen plunging toward the earth causing the pilgrims to scream in terror. When the sun eventually resumed its normal behaviour about twelve minutes after it began this mysterious display, these rain-soaked people found their clothing completely dry. Further, a number of pilgrims who came with medical problems found their ailments either completely healed or significantly alleviated. In addition, more than ten thousand people in the surrounding villages who chose not to go to the apparition site saw the sun dance in the sky. One of the principal anti-clerical publications of the day was *O Dia*, a major Lisbon newspaper. In the edition dated October 17th, *O Dia* reported the following:

> *At one o'clock in the afternoon, midday by the sun, the rain stopped. The sky, pearly gray in color, illuminated the vast arid landscape with a strange light. The sun had a transparent gauzy veil so that the eye could easily be fixed upon it. The grey mother-of-pearl tone turned into a sheet of silver which broke up as the clouds were torn apart and the silver sun, enveloped in the same gauzy grey light, was seen to whirl and turn in the circle of broken clouds. A cry went up from every mouth and people fell to their knees on the muddy ground. The light turned a beautiful blue as if it had come through the stained-glass windows of a cathedral and spread itself over the people who knelt with outstretched hands. The blue faded slowly and then the light seemed to pass through yellow glass. Yellow stains fell against white handkerchiefs, against the dark skirts of women. They were reported on the trees, on the stones and on the Serra. People wept and prayed with uncovered heads in the presence of the miracle they had awaited.*

The other major Lisbon newspaper, *O Seculo*, sent its editor, Avelino de Almeida to the scene. He had been quite dismissive of the entire story of Fatima and its predicted miracle in an article he wrote on the morning of the 13th. However, now a witness to the events of Fatima, he noted the following:

> *From the road, where the vehicles were parked, and where hundreds of people who had not dared to brave the mud were congregated, one could see the immense multitude turn toward the sun, which appeared free from clouds and in its zenith. It looked like a plaque of dull silver and it was possible to look at it without the least discomfort. It might have been an eclipse. But at that moment a great shout went up and one could hear the spectators nearest at hand shouting: "A miracle! A miracle!" Before the astonished eyes of the crowd, whose aspect was Biblical as they stood bareheaded, eagerly searching the sky, the sun trembled, made sudden incredible movements outside any cosmic laws—the sun "danced" according to the typical expression of the people.*

Another observer who witnessed these events was Joseph Garrett, a natural sciences professor at Coimbra University. Dr. Garrett described the events in a similar manner:

> *This was not the sparkling of a heavenly body, for it spun round on itself in a mad whirl, when suddenly a clamour was heard from all the people. The sun, whirling, seemed to loosen itself from The Firmament and advance threateningly upon the earth as if to crush us with its huge fiery weight. The sensation during these moments was terrible.*

I wasn't sure what to make of all these stories but I was getting excited at the prospect of visiting the area myself. I would have some free time, as my meeting with Sister Lucy was not until the following day.

After landing in Lisbon our flight was held up for some time on the tarmac. At first I thought nothing off it until some uniformed officers began boarding the plane. The senior flight attendant handed one of the officers a passenger list, which he in turn discussed with another officer. The two then started walking towards me and I was sure I was going to be arrested. I had no way of getting off the aircraft. One of the officers stopped at my aisle. He checked the overhead seat number before running his finger down the passenger list. He turned to his colleague and said something which brought him over to where I was seated. I tried not to look at them.

"You must come with us sir."

I just froze.

"Father, we have arranged a special vehicle for your children."

In showing my relief I almost did get arrested. One of the officers asked me if I was ok. I said that I was nervous from flying. He laughed and said that he also hated to fly. The local army had sponsored the priests' group and had arranged a special bus to help with those in wheelchairs.

I finally picked up my hire car and headed north for Fatima. I had pre-booked a room in Coimbra for that night so this left me three or four hours to spend in the town of Fatima itself.

Fatima is approximately 115km north of Lisbon. The drive was a good tonic to help me get over the shock of those army guys on the plane. I took in some of the scenery while at the same time I concentrated on the poorly kept roads. My mind wandered back over the events. First being hired, then the break in and the theft, and everything that followed. I hadn't seen the latest news as I couldn't find an English or Italian paper at the airport in Lisbon. I thought the coverage might not be so prolific outside of Rome or Italy and I was sure there would be little coverage of the mystery intruder in the foreign press.

I arrived in Fatima around noon and parked near the centre of town near where many of the tourist buses had already parked. The centre of Fatima, which was a larger town than I had expected, seemed to be one gigantic esplanade leading towards a church. The Basilica itself looked only small but with adjoining wings similar to that of Saint Peters in Rome. I decided to join one of the many tour groups after seeing an advertisement on a sandwich board near where I had parked. The tour would last around three hours and included a rest in a teahouse.

We set off to visit a series of shrines and holy places and I listened as the story of the three children was retold. I was now very familiar with the events of 1917 and found myself helping with little bits of information as the speaker paused from time to time. If this had been a school outing I would have been poking fun at the whole presentation. There were thirty or so in our group and despite a few language barriers, which caused the leader to have to repeat some things over, we had a great afternoon. We saw the homes of the three children and the group took pictures of the spot where Our Lady was said to have appeared. I was standing looking at a monument that was built to commemorate the events when a sense of irony came over me. I remember thinking how amazing all this was. As a child I had listened for hours to stories like this one, about miracles and visions in far off places and there I was on my very own pilgrimage to such a place. The greatest sense of irony came when we had entered the field where Our Lady appeared to the children and had performed the miracle. Our guide started to speak of the secret message Our Lady had given the children and how one part of the message had never been made public. The guide said that Lucia, who had since become Sister Mary Lucy had written the message down and it now resided in the holy city awaiting a decision by the Pope to make it known to all the world. She stammered as she said the word Pope realizing that Pope John Paul I, had only just died. She also said that perhaps the next Pope would reveal the 'secret message.' I had that very message in my jacket pocket.

I hadn't thought of that envelope all afternoon and once reminded, it made me paranoid again. Was I being followed? Maybe I was being minded rather than followed. I am glad that I visited the town. It made me look forward to meeting Sister Lucy even more. I was keen to solve the mystery of the letter and learn whether the information it contained could really bring down or damage the Catholic Church. But I also found myself being taken by the story. Did these kids really see Mary? Something happened here all those years ago, but visitations? It had a certain credibility to me just because of the location.

I hate the way that all UFO sightings happen in America. You have a group of aliens who have travelled for many years to get here and they only choose America, never Scotland or Tasmania. Still, Scotland has the monster I suppose and Tasmanians reckon they had a tiger once that was really a dog. Maybe this is what it's all about. The Yanks have aliens, the Scots have a monster and now the Portuguese have Our Lady. Is it just a tourist stunt taken to the maximum? There was something about Fatima that looked real. They hadn't built a Holiday Inn in the field and the souvenir vendors weren't tacky. I was slowly being converted. I wanted to believe the children more than I wanted to believe that the men who hired me had a good reason for doing so. Whatever the truth, the children didn't seem to benefit from all of this. Their own parents, though supportive, didn't actually believe what had happened. The local priest of the day didn't call them liars but told his own church seniors that he thought it was fake. Lucia asked the others not to mention what had happened after the first apparition but Jacinta couldn't help but tell her mum. There were lots of eyewitness accounts recorded in the local paper of the times and there were still many people alive in Fatima that remembered the events well. It happened only sixty-one years before my visit that day so most of the elders of the town would have been teenagers at the time. I was talking myself into being a supporter every minute I remained in the place. It reminded me a lot of Ireland. Green fields, stone fences and funny looking houses that last forever despite having no solid construction.

Someone tapped me on the shoulder, waking me from my daydream and I joined the others for the bus ride back to town. Before leaving Fatima I decided to buy myself a lasting memory of the place. I went into a small shop, which was really just part of a small home in the centre of town. Here they sold gift items, stationery, and souvenirs including photographs of the children. I bought some notepaper, a fountain pen, which had a picture of Our Lady etched on the side and a post card of Fatima. I also bought one picture of the three children together and three small individual prints of the children on their own.

The photographs, it was claimed, had been taken whilst Our Lady was actually appearing to the three shepherd children. I stared at the pictures for some time before allowing the shop assistant to place them into a bag for me. Now I knew that this was not a trick. The children most certainly were looking at something they thought special. You could never set up such photographs with children. Lucia was ten and the others were younger still with Jacinta being only seven years of age. No one could have asked her to fake something so grand. The ruthless grilling she received from village folk would have brought her undone.

The photograph of Francisco was the most telling. You could see the boy's soul through those eyes. Newspapermen tried to trick him and the others, as did men from the clergy. Their own family members would say to one of the children, 'oh come on, you can stop now; as we have heard the truth.' They would pretend that one of the children had owned up to the lie. This is a common tactic used by police. But still the children would not give it up. If it was a charade it was the greatest of all time. But the look on their faces, what had they seen?

I walked back to my car but had to wait several minutes while the many buses were boarded. Day-trippers by the thousand were leaving and the scene was a touch chaotic. I saw an elderly couple that had been in my tour group and we chatted for a while. They had been travelling all over Europe visiting religious shrines like this one. I thought they were trying to buy their way into heaven at the last minute. It was unfair of me to think that, as I knew nothing of their lives. The man asked me if I had been to the war. In my ignorance I said, "what war." The man's wife started to cry. It turned out that they had lost a son in Vietnam. He had been around my age. They had assumed I was American. They never got to say goodbye and it seems they couldn't let go. They weren't tourists. They were looking for answers.

CHAPTER 16

Coimbra was a reasonable sized town made up of a large number of narrow roads with no signposts. The hotel looked quite modern and I was keen to get to my room. I was tired from the long day and driving, which was hard going in the poorly maintained rental car. I liked the simple lifestyle of the province. Farmers would hold you up for ages while their sheep played around on the roads. On several occasions I had to wait while a couple of guys patched holes in the road by hand. I remember seeing two guys on the outskirts of Fatima who were mixing the tar in a big porridge bowl and then plying it on with what looked like a big wooden spoon. Once they finished they waived me through and I couldn't help thinking that they had probably spent their entire working life fixing the same stretch, over and over.

I had a great sleep that night. I dreamt of the apparitions and wondered if it was possible to stage such an event. If it was, you could make millions out of it. If I had only thought of this before my TV rental scam! Mind you, Ireland has had its fair share of visions. The South-West of Ireland is grotto city. Every few miles along the road there is a personal shrine to some great happening. I was relaxed. Thinking humorous things for the first time in ages. Maybe I could go back to Dublin and run some racket using all the skills I had acquired.

The big day had arrived. I would finally meet Sister Mary Lucy. I had breakfast around 6.30am and set off for Tuy. The drive was great with some fabulous views along the way. I saw the Atlantic Ocean many times as I made my way to Porto, and more road workers with their big porridge bowls. At one point I stopped to stretch my legs for a few minutes and was really struck by the beauty of the place. I promised myself I would go back there one day. I thought of Maria as I stood gazing at the great ocean. She loved the sea. She once told me that her dream home would be a shack on a remote beach far away from the entire world. I was still uneasy about our last conversation. I wondered why she had been so anxious when I spoke to her. I will call her, I thought, after I have seen the nun. I even went as far as to convince myself I would tell her the whole sordid story. I drove on to Braga and then finally to Tuy.

I crossed over an ancient looking bridge spanning the Mino River, which was also the border and headed for the town centre. The town was picture postcard stuff, with fabulous stone buildings and churches that looked hundreds of years old. It was early afternoon—the time Sister Lucy and I had agreed on. I was tired from the drive but keen to go straight to the convent. I stopped at a petrol station to fill up hoping to use the bathroom so that I could tidy myself up. I asked the garage attendant if he knew where the Dorothean Sisters convent was but he shrugged his shoulders and said, "not know." He didn't understand me. I had been given basic directions on the phone the day I made the appointment so I followed those.

The town was filled with churches and what could have been convents. I pulled up outside one that turned out to be a school and another that was actually a hospital or home for the aged. I left the main road and by chance found it in the first road I turned into. Standing just a short distance from the intersection was the convent of the Dorothean Sisters. There was a little shingle with weathered lettering hanging just outside the entrance. I suddenly got a knot in my stomach and sat in the car for a few seconds to compose myself. I studied the item I was to return one last time before checking my appearance in the rear view mirror. I walked up to the entrance and knocked on the big timber door. At first there was no response so I knocked again, this time looking behind me, gazing back along the road. There were no other cars, no people, I wasn't being followed. I had forgotten all about possible pursuers until now.

Suddenly a small viewing window opened from the centre of the door. I couldn't see in but I heard a voice.

"Can I help you senor?"

I was still trying to see in through the little window that had opened but the inside was too dark. I told the person that I had come to see Sister Lucy. I quickly corrected that and said it was Sister Mary Lucy.

"Hold there for one moment senor."

I didn't have to wait long and the door opened. There was a middle-aged lady in front of me. She was not dressed in nuns' uniform.

"Please senor to follow me."

She led me into what I assumed was a waiting room.

"Please senor to wait."

The room, which had a narrow doorway and a roof measuring barely six feet high, felt uncomfortable the moment I entered. It had every appearance of being a prison cell and I had half expected the door to slam shut behind me when my Spanish captor left. The woman had closed it very gently.

The walls were bare, save for a stone crucifix and little light was coming in from the two tiny windows. I sat down on the one chair in the room and wiped my forehead with my jacket sleeve. It was not a warm day, but I was feeling hot and I was starting to sweat. I couldn't hear any sounds coming from any of the surrounding rooms or the courtyard that I assumed was beyond the two windows, which were really just narrow slits cut through the stone wall. This silence only increased my anxiety. I guess I expected to hear singing or the sounds of children playing somewhere inside the grounds.

When I had visited the convent in Belfast it was full of sounds. There were children having choir practice and nuns running English classes for the local children of the many local single mothers.

I took off my jacket and told myself to relax. Given the time I'd had to prepare I hadn't decided what to say about the letter and how it had come to be in my possession. I peered down at the floors, which were bare timber but polished so that I could almost see my reflection in the panelling. Only pure devotion or grand punishment could maintain such a finish. Looking up I could see a small candle, set in a miniature grotto, which appeared to be chiseled into the plaster wall. It seemed to be the only source of light for evening time in the tiny room. Would I still be here when it required lighting? That thought entered my head more than once.

Of all the places to be held prisoner! In the country that gave a completely new meaning to pain. The Spanish have left a great legacy to all villains—don't get caught. I really didn't know anything about the Spanish inquisition. All I understood was that the Christian Spanish clearly didn't like the Jews.

I'd been in the room for only ten minutes but it felt like half an hour. I was trying my best to dream up some story about how I had obtained the letter. Surely I could concoct something. But she was a nun I thought, I shouldn't lie to her. Maybe I'll just say a friend gave it to me and I was doing him a favour. Christ that sounded weak. Then I thought about saying I was a cleaner in the Vatican and that I had found it. I didn't get a chance to continue this ludicrous conversation with myself as the lady returned to the room.

"Senor to follow me please."

I didn't say anything, just picked up my jacket and followed the woman. I moved out into the reception area, which I had only seen briefly on my arrival. Once inside the main entrance my eyes shifted to the vaulted ceiling supported by massive beams, no doubt designed to give any visitor a false sense of security before being placed in the stuffy confines of the waiting room. We walked down an impressive foyer, which led to a series of wooden stairs. Again the walls were bare except for the occasional grotto cut neatly out of the wall to create a small altar for candles. There were no statues and no grand paintings on display here. We took the downward staircase until we were at least two stories below the waiting room. We came to a long dark passage, which led to a number of small rooms that resembled prison cells from a medieval castle. I was taken to the end of the corridor and left alone to wait outside one of the rooms with no further instructions.

The air was very cool and again the place was filled with silence. I put my jacket back on. I stood to attention for a minute and then lent back against the wall. How in heaven's name did a mug like me end up in this situation? It was fantastic. The whole thing was so fantastic. I wished the lads were here. God, I would love to see their faces as we matched crime stories. The one miracle that had taken place was the fact that I hadn't told anyone about my life. If all these things had happened in Dublin everyone would have known. I was almost bursting at the seams feeling utterly chuffed with myself as I reviewed my body of work. But things were different here. I wasn't as prepared as I should have been. Would Sister Lucy understand English or Italian? I had tried to speak to the lady who let me in but she ignored me or didn't understand me. I hadn't thought about language. The Sister's accent was very strong on the phone and she had spoken in English. I thought about the young Lucia, her childhood given up to prayer. Being alone and hidden away from the local kids probably saved her life. I wondered what Francisco and Jacinta's lives would have been like had they not been taken so young. Jacinta looked so innocent. She was said to have been so completely overwhelmed at the beauty of the lady and I was saddened to think of her dying all alone in that Lisbon hospital. She must have been so desperately lonely at the end with none of her family or friends around her. Just to look at Jacinta's photo, her expression had really moved me. I found myself more of a believer having read the story of Jacinta Marto.

I went back to thinking about the letter and what I would say when the door behind me opened. I pushed myself off the wall and stood upright. The door had opened outward into the passageway and a short elderly lady in traditional nuns' dress was before me.

"Welcome senor." With this the lady moved back into the room, beckoning me with her hand to follow her.

CHAPTER 17

The lady sat down at a small table that had a single bench seat on either side. I was still looking at the few possessions around her, before she gestured that I be seated. I had to adjust the table slightly to make room for myself and as I did this I continued surveying the room. I noticed a photograph on a narrow shelf behind the tiny bed. It was set in a nice timber frame and had a set of rosary beads hanging from one corner. The woman noticed that I was looking at the photo and this was when our meeting really began. She smiled at me and began speaking of the two people in the black and white photograph.

"Beautiful children" she said after turning to look at the picture. "I wished Jacinta to be my sister, I love her so very much. I never see or hear the more loving one in all the world since."

The lady spoke with broken but clear English.

"Francisco was so peace…so much peace in his eyes, his mother and father so proud of him. They always proud for him." "Excuse…excuse," she exclaimed, "I am Sister Mary Lucy."

I interrupted before she could say anything more and apologized for not introducing myself first, to which she replied, "I know you Senor, I know." Once again I apologized and told her I was nervous.

"You are safe here, no have the fear," she assured me.

I told her that I had read all about Jacinta and Francisco and that I too had some photographs including one of Lucia. She almost looked embarrassed when I said this. I was glad that our first round of talks was idle chitchat because it helped me relax. I was surprised at her understanding of English though I did have to intersperse this with bits of Italian and some gestures.

I told the Sister that I had travelled up through Fatima and that I had visited the home of her birth. She asked me if there were many people passing through the little town. I said there were so many I couldn't find parking for my hire car. She looked proud at hearing this news. I was stumbling along trying to keep the talk neutral when she said, quite abruptly, "You come to give something senor? You say on telephone a package and a seal on the back. You have a package with you?" She said this with great anticipation. "Have you package here senor…for me?" I placed my hand inside my jacket and removed from the inner pocket a leather pouch. It had previously been used to hold my passport and some bank details. I carefully removed the envelope from the pouch and presented it to Sister Lucy. She didn't take it at first. She just wanted to look at it. Then she lifted one hand towards it and ran a finger along one edge. She lifted her other hand and carefully took the envelope from me. She placed it gently on our table with the seal upward.

"I write this letter here—this room, this table." She paused a little. "It so very hard to write and I be so frightened." She sat more upright as if preparing to tell a story. "The letter must be read long time ago, but this not happening." She afforded a tiny smile. "I am told that one Pope has read letter but has not to speak of it." She continued, "I was frightened for the words but Blessed Virgin Mary give me strength to write them. She is very sad that the world not hear this message." She looked disappointed at her own revelations of what was to have happened.

I had overheard Pope John Paul say that it was his intention to make public the words of the seer, so I can only assume he would have done this had he lived. I kept my resolve not to discuss the Pope's death with Sister Lucy as it was so completely tied to my having the envelope there that day.

I went to speak, "Sister…I."

"Please senor, please," she said, "no need to say anything of the return of this." She picked up the envelope and opened it very slowly. She touched the notepaper inside but didn't remove it from the envelope. "I thank you Senor for bringing this to me, now I am tired and I must rest if you please."

I felt dejected. Did I expect her to reveal this great mystery? She noticed that I was looking slightly agitated.

"Senor, I see you want for something?" She clasped her hands as though in prayer and placed her fingertips into her chin below her mouth. Then she spoke in a soft calming tone. "Senor, Our Lady gives me not to say the message, only give to Holy Father of church." She removed her hands from her face and took up the silver cross that hung from a set of rosary beads about her dress.

She continued speaking whilst looking at the cross now resting across her palm. "I tell the people the message is in the Bible. You must have the faith senor."

I had read about the message from Our Lady in a pamphlet handed out to me while on the tour in Fatima. The first part of the secret was a horrifying 'vision of hell' where the souls of sinners go and contained an urgent plea from Our Lady for acts of prayer and sacrifice to save souls. The second part of the secret specifically prophesized the outbreak of World War II and contained the mother of God's solemn request for the consecration of Russia as a condition of world peace. It also predicted the inevitable triumph of her immaculate heart. I could sense that Sister Lucy was about to stand and clearly our meeting was coming to an end but not before she would surprise me. "Senor I thank you once more, now I would like to give you something." With this she stood and walked the few steps to the little shelf, which housed the picture of Jacinta and Francisco Marto. She lifted the rosary beads that hung over the frames edge and handed them to me. "This belong to Jacinta, I have it all my life. I like you to look after it now." I was almost in pain with the sadness that filled me as she handed me this rosary. I looked at Lucia who had devoted her life to God. Would this woman become a saint one day? I didn't deserve any part of this. I was simply a common thief. God handpicked these children for their purity and innocence. I held out my hand and let the rosary fall gently into my palm.

Sister Lucy moved to the door and pushed it open, walked out into the passage and continued all the way to the staircase. I joined her at the foot of the stairs. She would not be leaving this floor. The lady who had shown me into the convent was now descending the stairs to collect me. Sister Lucy reached out to shake my hand and placed both her hands on mine. She didn't speak and she didn't look at me directly. I walked up the stairs and with my usher walked back to the main foyer. Suddenly I felt a desperate need to go back as she hadn't asked me how I had obtained it, nor had she checked its contents. By now I was at the main door. I turned back in the vain hope that Sister Lucy had come up the stairs but she hadn't. There were still no sounds anywhere in the building. The entrance door was open and I walked out under the low roof that protected the verandah. I turned around to see that the door had already been closed behind me. I hesitated for a moment before returning to my car still hoping to be summoned back.

I had driven all this way for such a short meeting and I had learned nothing. I still had no knowledge of who had hired me or what the letter meant to them or to the Vatican. I was more uncomfortable not understanding the great mystery of Fatima than I was worrying about Gelli, or whoever, coming after me.

CHAPTER 18

I left the car parked outside the convent and walked around the corner to a café, which had outside tables. I thought if anyone from the convent wanted me, they could see my car and know that I would be returning. I took an outside seat and ordered a local chicken dish and a glass of beer. I was quite hungry but needed the drink more than anything. It was getting late so I decided to find a room for the night, still hopeful that Sister Lucy might have more questions for me. I finished the meal and walked across the road to a quaint looking hotel. I booked a room and was able to park my car off-street behind the hotel. I had a shower and spent the evening lying on the bed watching crazy game shows and demolishing the mini bar. It took me a long time to go to sleep but the last mini scotch finally did the trick.

The next morning I had breakfast in the dining room of the hotel and checked to see if anyone had been asking after me. I packed the car with the few things I had with me and went to finalize the account. There was no one standing behind the counter so I rang the bell and waited. The reception area walls and foyer had been decorated with framed pictures of Tuy, which was a very attractive town. There were some original paintings on one wall depicting the surrounding area and these were for sale. On the side of the reception counter there was a large photograph of the convent I had visited the previous day. The photograph showed a large group of local school children with some of the Dorothean Sisters posing for the picture. I looked closely to see if I could recognize Sister Lucy but remembered that she actually lived in Coimbra now and had done so for about thirty years. I was sure that she must leave her own convent each year to prevent possible chaos from pilgrims wanting to meet with her during the October 13th anniversary.

I rang the bell again and called out a couple of times to attract the clerk who would fix up my account. A young girl opened the glass door behind the reception and made her way to the counter. She apologised for keeping me waiting and quickly prepared my account. I was still staring at the photograph of the convent when she said, "we will miss them."

"I'm sorry, you will miss who?"

"The Sisters, we will miss them."

I asked her what she meant, why would she miss them?

"The order, it has moved; the building it is now empty, it is very sad."

In a heartbeat I left the hotel, ran across the road and back towards the street where the convent stood. I sprinted round the corner, across the street and up to the convent entrance and banged on the door. I banged again and again. No answer. There was an old man watering some shrubs along the front of the building. I ran up to him and asked, "where are the Sisters, the Sisters...where are the Sisters?" He didn't understand me. I ran around to the side of the building but it was a stark wall with only tiny slits near the top for windows. I ran back around to the front and continued to the far side, again no sign of other doors. There was no access to the rear of the building, which was set behind a tall stone wall. The wall looked like it ran all the way from one side across the back of the grounds and around again to the other side in a semicircle.

I was out of breath and feeling giddy. I ran back to the entrance again and thumped on the heavy timber door but I knew no one would respond. I knew what had happened the second the girl in the hotel spoke. I had set up stings like this myself. I sat down on the doorstep, rested my head in my hands and thanked god that I hadn't fallen for it.

I had used the notepaper and fountain pen that I had purchased in Fatima to prepare a fake. I had taken the real note with me to the meeting at the convent but I had already placed my own note inside the envelope. Only the real author would know that mine was a forgery. The lady I met didn't actually look at the writing, only the paper. I couldn't be one hundred percent sure that the meeting was legitimate. I was hoping the sister would say that the note was a forgery and to that I would have responded by producing the original. Even though she said nothing I still wasn't convinced as to her identity. The words I wrote were in Portuguese and I had copied them from a tourist guide brochure found in my Hotel room in Coimbra. I wished I could see the look on Gelli's face as he had them interpreted.

I must have sat on that convent doorstep for an hour before I could move. The building was truly empty. I picked myself off the floor and went to get some coffee at the same café I had visited the previous day. I tried to strike up a conversation with the lady who brought the coffee but she understood no English and very little Italian. The coffee went cold while I stirred it a hundred times. The lady came back to see if I wanted anything else but she could see I hadn't touched the coffee and left me alone.

I paid for the drink and moved back out onto the tiled pavement. It was a pretty street with lots of trees and manicured garden beds. The few people I could see, were taking their time. A car passed me travelling all of ten miles an hour and even a dog was moving in slow motion up the main road. I was in no rush to leave Tuy. I had no back up plan, and nowhere to go.

My car was still parked at the rear of the hotel so I ambled across the street and walked back into the reception area. There were no guests and no one waiting at the counter. I stopped to look at the photograph again. There was a date in the bottom right hand corner, October 59'. Some of the children were dressed in their communion clothes. I could see some of their parents, who had crept into the side of the photo. The children were all smiling and I remembered my own special day at St Margaret's. Holy communion was a big event in Ireland. It was a bit like a wedding, all the relatives turned out. There was always a big spread at the end of it and I felt important in my brand new longers. While looking at the faces of the parents I saw a face I recognized. It was Gelli. He was much younger looking, but it was him standing to the side looking proudly over toward the children. He was standing behind a tallish lady and had his left hand resting on her shoulder, as though he was on tiptoes trying to gain a better view. The children were in rows of sorts and Gelli seemed to have his head tilted slightly to one side to see around a child standing near the second row. I ran my eyes along this row and soon found another familiar face. Much harder to recognize as this was a child, now a woman. I had no chance of seeing this face earlier because I wasn't really looking at the faces of the children. She must have been twelve or thirteen when the photograph was taken but her features were unmistakable. It was Olivia.

Now I was scared and very nervous. I didn't know what the relationship between her and Gelli was. All I knew was that the sweet little girl in the photograph worked as the receptionist for the firm in New York. I stared at her image and tried to come to terms with the fact that I had been set up over such a long period. I don't know how they did it but it was brilliant.

Standing there alone, disturbed momentarily by a cleaner who placed fresh flowers on the foyer's one small table, I received the worst shock of all. One more face amongst all this innocence for me to recognize. Standing on Olivia's left with a portion of her face hidden was a young and very innocent looking, Maria Del Vecio.

The receptionist returned to the front counter and I apologized for leaving earlier and quickly paid the account. I walked slowly through to the rear of the hotel and back towards my hire car. I paused to picture the scene all those years ago taking place practically across the road from where I stood. A group of young children making their Holy Communion or Confirmation. Olivia and Maria looking very pretty in their best frocks smiling for the camera.

The only thing left for me to do was to return the original note to the real Sister Lucy. I started the car and headed back to Coimbra. Despite being fooled by Maria whom I was certain had played a role, I wasn't feeling bitter towards her. I was glad however, that my streetwise instincts had prevented me from being completely turned over by her. If she hadn't liked me much all along, I was sure that she hated me by now.

The whole saga had become so complex, but as I drove I reminded myself over and over that I had stolen the letter and the Pope had been murdered, most likely by one of Gelli's people. Perhaps the Pope was going to bring an end to the corruption and this could have affected the firm somehow. When learning about the freemason group led by Gelli I did learn that some of the Vatican clergy themselves were accused of belonging to P2. I couldn't understand this because the Vatican prohibited priests from joining freemason groups. I had read that any priest found belonging to such an organization would face ex-communication. How could someone be a priest and be a freemason? If there really were Masons and other groups prevailing inside the Holy City it would be very difficult to eradicate them. The church has enough of its own legitimate factions to worry about. The selection of the Pope is a process in lobbying various groups for support. No doubt the incumbent would make a series of promises to gain the votes required to get the top job. The eventual victor would then spend half his term trying to back out of deals. Even the sharing of information within this Roman enclave is a nightmare in administration. Many of the sacred documents stored in the Vatican are stored in sections, with each factional group having access to only one portion. This is supposed to maintain the harmony between the groups. I am not sure it is working.

Maria had taught me most of what I knew about the Vatican. I couldn't see why she had bothered giving me lectures about the politics as we toured there together. I was almost feeling sorry for her. Everyone has their price I told myself, including me. Gelli must have been convinced that the secret message from Our Lady would fetch millions at a private auction. I started laughing, thinking how stupid, or more likely, how furious he would be when he learned the truth about his precious envelope and its phony contents.

I had now burned Gelli on two separate occasions. There was still the matter of the files I stole in Tottenham, London. These were still sitting in a safety deposit box and contained enough good news to undo a number of his mates. I was glad I had kept them. I had clearly put myself in danger but they might also provide a bargaining tool at some point.

The trip back to Coimbra seemed much shorter than I had remembered. The town is set on both sides of the river Mondego. A sign on its outskirts said the population was 90,000 people. Narrow streets separated the houses that were tightly but neatly packed together. The most famous building in Coimbra is the university and its bell tower can be seen from many different points around the town. I was able to get a room at the same hotel I had used a few days earlier and was grateful to have a hot shower and relax. I had another look at Lucia's letter and wished that I could read it. I thought about calling room service and simply asking someone to translate it to me. However, I thought better of that just on the off chance that it contained some diabolical news. I placed the two pieces of paper into the centre of one of the books I had purchased. The paper was delicate and I wanted to preserve it. I placed the book behind the wardrobe in my room and got ready to go out.

It was early evening and quite mild and there were a number of tourists filling the many restaurants and bars. I found a seat at a bar near the hotel and ordered a beer and a simple meal of Nabada a moda de Coimra, a dish of turnips, bread of maize and garlic. (I didn't know this when I ordered it). I overheard a group of people speaking of their great day in Fatima, sharing stories each giving their own synopsis of the apparitions. I met a young couple having a counter meal at the bar who had also spent the day touring Fatima. They weren't Catholics but they were interested in learning about the apparitions of 1917. I joined them for a while and they were amazed at how much I knew. I had a good time that evening chatting with tourists and finding some more agreeable food before wandering back to my hotel.

CHAPTER 19

It was Sunday and I woke to the sound of church bells, lots of church bells and all playing different tunes. I decided to go for a walk by the river, which was close by the hotel. It was about 8am and there were already a number of people in the street. There was a craft market and it attracted locals and tourists alike. The market stretched the length of the street and some stalls were set up on the bank of the river. Most of the items were hand made but there were people selling books and souvenirs. There was a stall selling religious artifacts such as bottles of holy water from a spring near Fatima. The water was most likely from a leak in someone's back garden but faith is a placebo, so maybe it does some good. I always think of my dad when I see a collection of holy items. If he had been there we would have needed a carry bag to take away our selection.

There was an old couple cooking a local breakfast dish on a barbecue by the river. About 20 local people were queuing there so I assumed it must be good. It wasn't. It was worse than the turnip meal from the previous evening. I ate what I could and then sat and watched as young men rowed boats in the fast moving Mondego. After breakfast I went back to my room, showered and got ready to go looking for Sister Lucy's convent.

There were many churches in the town and all were being filled ready for 9am mass. It appeared that everyone in Coimbra was going to church so I decided to do the same. I attended a small church preferring this to an almost Cathedral size place near my hotel. The sermon was in Portuguese and Latin and I understood none of it. The little church was popular with the local nuns, many of them occupying seats in the upper gallery. There was an organist performing hymns and the congregation sang beautifully. I was seated about midway and close to the wall. Around me were devout Catholics many of whom were not only attending this mass but also saying private rosary.

As I sat there that day listening to the beautiful words spoken by the priest I recalled the stories of the three young children of Fatima. I had studied the photographs of the children several times no doubt looking for a hint of fraud, but there wasn't any. I reached into my pocket and felt the rosary that the imposter had given me in Tuy. I still held them precious despite knowing that Jacinta had never owned them. I thought about the demands of Our Lady in wanting Russia to be consecrated and returned to her immaculate heart. I wondered why the church had taken no notice of the warning given to them by Sister Mary Lucy.

I hadn't noticed the congregation stand and a lady behind me tapped me on the shoulder no doubt to suggest that I did. As I stood I turned around to acknowledge my tardiness. My eyes strayed to the balcony and there I saw a man sitting amongst the sisters. He was seated at the end of the aisle nearest to the staircase. He was wearing a monk's robe, which he adjusted the moment I looked up. I recognized his face immediately, even from a distance. I remembered his features well from the previous time I had seen his face, from the safety of my hideout in his apartment. It was Albino Luciani, better known to the world as Pope John Paul.

I turned back and thanked God that he was still alive but now I had more questions than ever. There was no official press release because there was no body, murdered or otherwise. Albino must have escaped the Holy City fearing his life was in danger. He had only been Pope for little over a month. This was staggering news. It was all I could do to stop myself staring back. The mass was coming to an end. The people stood one last time and as I joined the congregation I looked up once more towards the balcony. He was standing, preparing to leave.

I was able to move along the side wall to the rear of the church and I waited until the man came down the spiral stairs. Unaccompanied, he walked out of the church and into the street. He crossed the road and headed up a slight incline towards the university. He turned into a lane-way that divided a small shopping strip and moved quickly to the far end. It looked like it was a dead end but there was a small flight of stairs that took him down to an adjoining lane-way. I was careful not to make too much noise on the metal staircase but I didn't want to lose sight of him. As soon as I reached the bottom of the stairs I realized where he was headed. I saw a sign which read 'Convent of the Carmelite Nuns.'

He stopped at a side entrance and waited. He didn't knock on the door or call out. I was able to get a position, which gave me full view of the door while keeping myself from view. The door suddenly opened and the man was gone. I couldn't believe what I had just seen. The Holy Father, still the pontiff of Rome had staged his own death and was here in Coimbra. He knew Sister Lucy. He had said so that night when I broke into his apartment. I walked to the end of the lane-way and made my way around to the main entrance of the convent. It was all I could do to stop myself from waltzing in and introducing myself. I didn't have the note with me and I needed to give some thought to what I had just witnessed. I wasn't sure if this changed anything. The story was fantastic. I could have made millions by selling the story to the world's press. I wouldn't do this however, as I had come to believe the story of Fatima. I believed the Holy Father must have been in danger to leave Rome as he did and travel to Portugal. It would have been harder for him to get out of the Vatican than it was for me to get in. It would have also been quite difficult for him to get to Portugal, even by car without being recognized. Still, he had only been Pope for a short time and this would be in his favour while moving around. It was quite likely that very few people, including the nuns in the convent, could say for sure that they knew who this man was. I would need to be very careful now in gaining a meeting with Sister Lucy. She would be very protective of her friend, a man who had obviously given her support.

I left the convent and walked back to the town. I had a coffee and then made my way back to the hotel. I felt strangely ecstatic at the events unfolding before me and felt like calling my dad. I knew he would have been devastated by the death of the Pope and I promised myself that I would inform him soon enough, hopefully face to face.

However, I did call Maria. That idea hit me suddenly. If she answered the phone I was going to say I knew everything and make fun of what happened to Gelli. The operator couldn't connect me, saying the line was disconnected. The whole thing was staged, Maria, her family, all of it. I knew this but still felt stupid. I had hoped that somehow she was also duped. But she must have known everything. Apart from Olivia, I could only wonder at who else might have been involved.

CHAPTER 20

I had been wrong in thinking that Sister Lucy abandoned Coimbra during the anniversary of the miracle of Fatima. She played a major role in the celebrations. I found a leaflet in the hotel lobby promoting the upcoming event on October 13th. There was a picture of Sister Lucy on the front of the flyer and I remember wishing I had seen this before going to Tuy. The woman who played the role of the nun during the sting in Spain looked nothing like her. I could see the resemblance to the young Lucia. The liner notes said that the one remaining seer would lead a procession in Fatima where a special mass would be held. It was now less than a week away, but I wanted to see Sister Lucy much sooner if I could. I knew that there would be thousands attending the anniversary and it would be very difficult to get near this woman whom many now regarded as a living saint. I would try to contact her at the convent.

On Monday morning I made my way to a small coffee shop that allowed me a look at the main entrance to the convent. I sat for some time observing the coming and going of the many visitors. The building was a school of sorts with many young ladies arriving early that day to attend class. The convent also received a number of deliveries during the morning. There were flowers followed by two separate food vans that unloaded what appeared to be general groceries. The next caller was the mailman. He arrived on foot having walked the short distance from the main Coimbra post-office. He was carrying a large sack of mail. He was well known to the Sisters so it would have been difficult for me to fake a late personal mail delivery.

I didn't want to give Sister Lucy prior knowledge of my visit. If she mentioned to Albino Luciani that someone claiming to have her letter was here in

Coimbra he may take flight. He must be on the run for his life, why else would a Pope fake his own death?

I wasn't that interested in Albino Luciani. I really just wanted to return the letter to its rightful owner and leave. Maybe he finally saw the light after getting the top job. It might be like being the President of the United States. The day you get the gig some guy comes to see you and informs you about everything from JFK to Roswell. You are supposed to keep the silence alive. Maybe Albino had the visit and didn't like what he heard.

I observed the convent and could see that there was little, if any, security. I had a good view of the entrance area as the double entrance doors were left open most of the day. I didn't want to get too close to the building and risk attracting attention to myself. I noticed that a number of tourists came by the convent and stopped to take pictures. Some of the tourists tried to enter the convent but were soon escorted out by one of the nuns. I kept my surveillance sessions short, as I wanted to observe a full day at the convent.

As evening fell there were still students arriving to attend the convent. This now included males. The ages of the students varied a great deal with many being mature aged. I spotted a group leaving around 9pm and decided to follow them. The group, which consisted of two men and three women, visited a local restaurant. I waited until they were seated and then went in and found a seat on the adjoining table. They were all students at Coimbra University. One of the three girls was Italian another Spanish and the remainder of the group were Portuguese. The Italian girl was doing her best to speak some Portuguese but had to continually prompt herself in Italian. They finished their meal and three of the group left the restaurant. The two remaining ordered coffees and I used this opportunity to introduce myself. The Italian girl had stayed along with a local boy. I struck up a conversation by asking how they enjoyed studying at the university. The young man could speak a little English but I was directing my exchange to the girl. She was around 25 years of age. She was very friendly and told me that she was studying theology. She had chosen Coimbra University because she also wanted to study Portuguese and Spanish. The young man decided to leave. The girl was about to leave with him when I asked if she would keep me company and tell me more about Coimbra and her studies. She agreed to stay. The young chap kissed her on the check and she said she would see him in class tomorrow.

We were alone and I formally introduced myself. I told her I was on holiday and had been touring around southern Spain and now Portugal. Her name was Rebecca. I remember that first meeting like it was yesterday. Rebecca was so pretty with beautiful long dark straight hair, which was draped around one shoulder. She had lovely soft brown eyes and perfect white teeth. I spoke to her for a while about her studies and then asked her what she knew about Coimbra and the surrounding area. She spoke mainly about the religious history of the region. Her studies focused on events such as the Spanish inquisition and the progress and survival of Christianity. She had also studied the local apparitions. Rebecca told me the story of Lucia, Francisco and Jacinta. From the way she relayed it I had little doubt that she believed it. She was very passionate about the apparitions and indicated how wonderful it would be to see Our Lady. I thought she may have chosen Coimbra University because of its location to Fatima and the fact that Sister Lucy was living there. I was careful not to show my knowledge of the events and she seemed to enjoy re-telling the story.

Rebecca had become an expert on Fatima. She knew all the facts as I had read them and many more. She spoke of the anger she had towards the Vatican for not taking the message of Fatima seriously. She told me a funny story about how the local authorities had kidnapped Lucia before one of the apparition appointments in an effort to stop the charade. The towns' folk marched on the major's office demanding that she be released. She was only ten years old and being held like a criminal. She was released immediately and the people marched along with Lucia to the field just in time for her meeting with the Blessed Virgin Mary. Jacinta who was already waiting at the spot along with Francisco said, "its ok, Lucia is here now." Lucia apparently apologized to Our Lady for being late. Rebecca had become a little teary eyed as she told me this story. She laughed to compose herself. I didn't have to encourage Rebecca, she was keen to talk and express her views. She then surprised me by saying she didn't even think the Pope was dead. This was so out of context to our conversation. She told me that a family member, who was a priest in Rome, indicated that Pope John Paul was always going to struggle because of his anti-corruption views. She suggested that the new Pope could have threatened arrangements that were lining the pockets of powerful men in the holy city. She suspected that Pope John Paul could disappear quite easily as he had been the Pope for such a short time and wouldn't be easily recognized. She didn't know just how right she was. I had been to church with his Eminence the previous morning.

I said I would travel to Fatima and have a look around, as I was interested in the story that she had just told me. She said, "you can meet one of the Fatima children here in Coimbra." I asked her how that could be. She explained that the children were still very young in 1917 and that the one surviving member of the trio was now a nun in her seventies and living in a convent in the town. Rebecca told me that she had met Sister Lucy on several occasions when she lectured to groups taking religious studies at the convent. She explained that the Sister was very outspoken on matters of the modern church and was not the timid nun her demure appearance suggested.

It was late and Rebecca said she needed to leave as she had class at 9am the following day. I told her where I was staying and asked if I could escort her home as it wasn't out of my way. She smiled and agreed, knowing that it was in the opposite direction to my hotel. She lived in a guesthouse near the university about ten minutes walk from the restaurant. I told Rebecca that I was glad to have met with her and asked if she would have dinner with me the following evening. She agreed. As we said goodnight I kissed her on the cheek. She laughed and said she thought only Italian men did that sort of thing. The door to the guesthouse opened and I caught the stare of an overseer. Rebecca gave me one more smile and marched in. I walked back to the main street, had a beer and went back to my hotel. I was feeling very confident about returning the letter to Sister Lucy but had no idea how I would actually do this. I ran through a number of ideas but had to consider Albino. Any approach I took to see Sister Lucy may have been seen as a potential attack on the Pope. I had to see her face to face, no introduction, no warning.

CHAPTER 21

❀

I was woken from a deep sleep by a loud banging noise. The thumps got louder and louder and I could hear a woman's voice yelling, get up…get up. I told her to hang on, threw a towel around myself and made my way to the door. As I unlocked the door she burst into the room almost knocking me over. I regained my balance and turned to find Rebecca standing in my room.

"It was you." She held up a newspaper and shoved it towards me. "It was you, wasn't it? Who are you, tell me before the police get here."

She looked wild. "Calm down…just calm down," I tried my best to soothe her, all the while thinking she was about to smash me one.

She swore at me and swore again this time throwing the paper at me.

"Have you called the police?" I asked.

She didn't respond. She was standing close to me. I reached out and took her hands and asked her again. "You said, before the police get here."

"I didn't contact anybody…but I wish I had!"

I pulled her closer.

She asked me again, "who are you?"

Rebecca had been reading a copy of the local paper from Rome. The issue was a few days old. She had read the story about the man seen at the Vatican and recognized me immediately from an artist's impression that accompanied the article. It was a good likeness. No doubt Maria had supplied someone a photograph of my good self. I asked Rebecca to sit down. I tidied up the bed-clothes and she sat on the corner of the bed. I couldn't tell what time it was. I poured her a glass of water. She took a gulp and asked me if I was going to hurt her. I was quite shaken by this. I told her not to be frightened and that she was in no danger. She told me how she had started reading the paper in bed, not long after I had walked her home. She had some newspapers sent to her every week by her family. She told me that she couldn't believe her eyes when she saw my face beaming out from her local paper. The man who had walked her home in the dark only minutes earlier was seen at the Vatican the night the Pope was murdered.

I told Rebecca the whole story, everything from Dublin to New York to Rome. I told her about Maria and Gelli and how I had been set up to be implicated in the Pope's death. I told her about the envelope belonging to the Fatima girl and how I was conned in Tuy. By now she was just gazing at me eyes wide open and mouth ajar.

"You stole…the secret message…from Our Lady?" She stood up, slowly turning to face me. Fists clenched, face now twisted with anger, eyes piercing. "Have you any idea…you stupid moron…how important that artifact is to Catholic people?" She spoke to me as though I 'was' a moron and continued hurtling abuse like pathetic imbecile as she spun around my room.

"Rebecca, they didn't get the letter, they really didn't…I have it here." She regained her composure and almost whispering said, "Please…don't play games, may I see it." I asked her to sit back down. I reassured her that the letter was safe. I told her that I no longer had the envelope but the original note was safe. I retrieved it from its hiding place and sat down next to her. I wiped my hands on the bed sheet, opened the book and passed the letter to Rebecca. She held it like a fragile leaf. Her eyes widened in anticipation as she unfolded the paper.

"The writing…it's strange." She said. "Some Portuguese and old letters…like ancient writing, Hebrew, maybe Aramaic." She looked up for confirmation. "I have studied some early Christian text." She paused, looking at me again as though seeking encouragement. "Few people here could translate this." She didn't seem disappointed at not being able to read all of it. She studied the second page and then returned to the first. I told her the pages were in the order I found them. It was difficult to say which was which. She placed the two pages together again, placed them back down in the centre of the book, and clasped her hands together. "Hail Mary full of grace."

Rebecca recited the entire prayer and blessed herself. She looked a little embarrassed at her actions.

"The name of the Pope and the date are precise," she explained. "Though Sister Lucy wrote this in 1944 it contains the exact date that the pages were to be viewed, and by whom."

Rebecca told me that in 1959 Pope John XXIII had called for the envelope containing the message to be delivered to him. A witness had made it known that on August 20, 1959 Pope John XXIII had opened the envelope in his presence. "He must have gotten a terrible shock to see his own name written clearly in the note." Rebecca flopped back onto the bed. Lying there with her hands over her face she said, "this is unbelievable, totally unbelievable."

I told her to brace herself because it gets better. "The Pope…he's not dead." She pulled herself upright.

"Where, I mean how, where is he, how do you know?"

"He's here…in Coimbra."

She looked ecstatic and she looked beautiful. My heart was beating so fast. I just wanted to kiss her there and then.

"What's wrong?" she asked.

"Nothing, nothing." I had been staring at her. I turned away and apologized. She lifted the book up off my lap and placed it gently onto the floor. Rebecca then turned towards me, threw her arms around me and gave me a fierce hug. She said that she was sorry for accusing me. I told her that if she was going to make up by doing that, she should accuse me of something else. We both laughed.

Rebecca wanted to know what my plans were. I told her that I wanted to give the letter back to Sister Lucy. She was happy with that. She took my hands squeezed them tightly then pleaded, "can I help you, please, please…please?" I said I hadn't decided how or when I would see Sister Lucy but that I would let her help if possible. I suggested that she had better go home. She stood up and walked toward the door. She flicked one light switch down opening the light to the bathroom and then turned off the main room light. She walked back towards me and standing in front of me said, "I am staying." There was an awkward silence and I realized that I had somehow overwhelmed Rebecca. I told her that she could stay and I went into the bathroom so that she could undress. I reminded myself that I really liked this girl and that she was only staying because she didn't want to get into trouble with her landlady who was sure to catch her coming home at such an hour. When I returned to the bedroom I picked up a pillow and suggested that I would sleep on the floor, but Rebecca said that was silly and asked me to lie down and tell her more about my life. We talked for what seemed like hours, but eventually fell asleep.

I woke first and tried not to move as Rebecca was still sound asleep. She had kicked off most of the blankets so I tried to gently pull the sheet up to cover her. Just as I did this she woke to catch me looking at her almost naked body. She smiled, and pulled the sheet up herself. I asked her if she was going to school. She whispered back, "I think I'd better go to confession."

I used to hate confession as a kid. It seemed stupid to me. You do something wrong, go tell the priest and he forgives you for it, then you go and do it again. One time I told Father Nightingale that I stole money from the plate. I would put in sixpence and take out half a crown. He left his side of the confessional, burst into mine and gave me a clout around the head. Then he threw me out. As I was running down the aisle he said, "I'll tell your old man ya shagger." The confessional is supposed to be sacrosanct. Obviously not on Farley Hill.

Rebecca didn't want to leave. She said that she was worried I would disappear. I held her and promised her that I would not be leaving and so we made arrangements to meet again that evening.

CHAPTER 22

I was really happy I'd met Rebecca and was already desperate to see her again. I had never felt that way about Maria. I lay in bed all morning almost forgetting why I was in Coimbra. I finally got up, showered and dressed and went out to get something to eat. I thought about doing some shopping, maybe buy a little gift for Rebecca to make up for causing her such upset the previous night. I was being very casual and the day was running away when I thought of something that simply hadn't occurred to me before. Pope John Paul must know that the envelope was stolen. He would have known where it was kept hidden and would surely have tried to take it once he had decided to run away. He would have alerted Sister Lucy to this fact by now and I wondered if this would force her to reveal the message herself. The church had let her down by not revealing its contents and now she might think it was in the hands of a collector.

If it was Gelli who had planned the theft he now had to contend with a dud. But this wouldn't stop him from passing it off as authentic. I thought that Gelli might get someone to write a fake 'secret message' before selling it on to some dealer. Sister Lucy would have to be concerned that a fake could appear. This was something else that I had not considered. Gelli did have the original envelope. It would be easy to write some dramatic piece and that could be very damaging. I thought Gelli would be really pissed with me. Someone had wanted that letter real bad. I felt a sense of urgency and went straight back to the hotel.

I was desperate to meet Sister Lucy and needed something foolproof that would force her to see me no matter what her concerns. I went through the process, all the what, ifs, buts and maybes—no margin for error. I reminded myself of what had happened to me in Tuy…all my experience, yet still fooled.

A couple of times I thought I had the right idea but then found too many reasons for failure. I wanted Sister Lucy to leave the convent on her own and meet me. I thought about the little church where I had attended Mass the previous Sunday. A church was the one place a nun was sure to visit. How could I get the Sister to attend this church at a time designated by me? Finally the answer! It was a simple idea but I was confident it would work.

Rebecca came to my hotel around 6pm, much earlier than we had arranged. She was very affectionate towards me from the moment she arrived and said that she had missed me. I returned her hug and kissed her gently on the cheek. I loved the way she tried to speak English forgetting that I understood her Italian well enough. I had met a woman I could trust. I had also met a woman I could fall in love with, if I hadn't already.

I explained to Rebecca that I needed to deliver a note to Sister Lucy. I gave her some notepaper and asked her to copy down the section from Lucia's letter that had been written in Portuguese. When she finished I dictated a few more words and again Rebecca wrote these down in Portuguese. She checked her work several times before handing me the single sheet of paper.

That night Rebecca and I had some dinner in town and then sat by the river for a while. It was a nice evening. The sky was ablaze with stars. We spoke of love and miracles. She told me about the one man she had been serious with and I told her it would be a miracle if I ever trusted another woman after being stitched up by Maria. We laughed as we listened to each other reminisce. Rebecca told me about her teaching aspirations and how she hoped one day to get work in Spain or Portugal. She spoke of her religious beliefs and then in the same breath, her suspicions. She had little time for the Vatican. She told me stories of corruption that had proven to be true but had resulted in no Vatican official being charged. She had a strong faith in God but didn't see a role for the church. She told me how Jesus had said that the kingdom of God was in all of us. She concluded that the Vatican had no right to claim to be the seat of power. She pointed to a small house on the river front and said, "that house there has as much right to be the Vatican as does any building." I didn't offer her my own version of faith. I had always accepted what Father Nightingale told us. If you're good you go to heaven and if you're bad you'll burn in hell till all your skin melts off. I got in trouble with the good father during a RI lesson. We were talking about heaven and hell. I said I would hate to go to hell because it would be so cold. He scowled at me and said, "how could it possibly be cold in hell." I said, "because you wouldn't get near the fire for vicars." He had slapped me around the face for that. Sister Rita, head of torture for the little Sisters of Mercy, also slapped me around the face.

Hand in hand we walked back to the hotel and Rebecca stayed the night. I wasn't sure if she really liked me or if she just couldn't resist the opportunity to be involved with someone who was carrying a message from Our Lady.

I never had any great confidence with women. I always felt like they were after something other than my good looks, which were in short supply. But if anyone was using in this situation it had been me. I'd followed Rebecca that night, striking up conversation just to find out about the convent. She was with me for whatever reason, and I couldn't complain.

Rebecca left early the next morning and wished me luck. She knew what I was planning to do, and like me, was confident that it would work. I was ready early, and left the hotel to start work on my plan.

Saint Dominique's Church was a five-minute walk from my hotel. It was a small but graceful looking building, with its own belfry. Like many of the buildings in Coimbra its walls were stone, complemented with a stone fence. I was there to find out the hours of business. I called at the vestry adjoining the main structure and met with the cleaner. She said, "this church she never close for ever." I double checked the times shown for mass printed on a board affixed to the church door and found the confessional session times. This is where I would meet with Sister Lucy. I only had to figure out a suitable time.

I had the note that Rebecca had written and had to deliver it. I had come so far and the final plan was simple. I needed a disguise. The best disguise is often the most blatant as people are reluctant to dismiss officialdom. I was to be a priest, another reason for my visit to the church that morning. At the rear of the church I found all I needed to emerge as Father Shamus Flynn from dear old Ireland. I'd noticed at the Mass on Sunday that the parish priest and I were of similar build and I cut a fine figure in my new blacks. My dad would have killed me with his bare hands if he'd seen this one.

The convent was busy. There were young novices filing around the place and mother superior types floating as only a nun can. I entered the Convent bold as brass and didn't attract any attention. The reception desk looked like a typical hotel desk. I approached the young novice. "My name is Father Shamus Flynn from Dublin. I have an envelope for Sister Mary Lucy. Can you tell me if she is here in the building today?" The young nun hadn't moved an inch whilst I spoke. Then she raised her palm to me as if to say hold please. She left, I hoped, to get someone to assist me. She returned with another youngish nun who introduced herself by telling me she spoke English. I repeated my earlier announcement to which she replied. "Yes sir, Sister Mary Lucy is in private prayer this morning." I told the nun that the bishop of Lisbon had asked me to deliver this envelope in person to the convent. I explained that I couldn't wait to see Sister Lucy myself as I had a talk to give at the university shortly. I further informed the young lady standing in front of me that the bishop had asked me to ensure that the envelope was taken to the Sister the instant it arrived. The young nun took the envelope from me and promised it would be handed to the Sister immediately. I added one more thing. "Please tell the Sister that the priest who delivered the envelope requested that you read it immediately. He expects that you will want to respond this morning." I thanked her for her assistance and left the reception area and returned to the street.

I wandered slowly back to the church and waited. I didn't know for sure how long it would take Sister Lucy to arrive but I knew she would come. I changed back into my own clothes, which I had hidden, and took a seat at the front of the church. I stared up at the big stone crucifix and said a private 'forgive me' prayer. One minute you don't believe in God, then you see a big stone crucifix and you do again, like magic. It's like when I visited friends' houses as a kid. I would be on my way out the door, see the holy water and bless myself, always. All the homes in Ireland had a little grotto full of holy water just near the front door. Even if you were going out robbing you would still bless yourself, always. Sometimes I made fun of people blessing themselves after I had already done it on the slight. There's something about relics and crucifixes and holy water that makes you have no doubt.

I heard footsteps and turned to see the cleaner entering the church. She went straight through to the priests changing area off to the side of the altar. Then an old man meandered in. He said a couple of prayers and was gone again. Two elderly ladies appeared, lit candles, and they too were soon gone. I started humming hymns. I was a great singer as a kid. It was difficult to be a great singer and a skinhead at the same time. I would tell my mates I was held back in detention but was really doing choir practice. Being in the choir meant getting heaps of time off Math and English and you also got to mix with the good looking girls. The best lookers were the tryhards and they were always in the choir. Normally they wouldn't give me the time of day but in the choir I was an equal so I got to know them quite well. I started seeing one for a while; she was my first love. She said I could sing great and asked me to sing at her house while her mother played the piano. I only did this once. I went to kiss her and the next day she gave me a tube of toothpaste with a note. I read the note but I didn't use the toothpaste.

I waited ages. I hated having to rely on someone else to do my work but in this case I had no choice. I had to tell Sister Lucy something that would guarantee she would see me. The church had a slow stream of visitors. Most lit candles, some prayed. The cleaner was long gone and I hadn't seen the parish priest so I guessed the pubs must be open. I walked around the church and even walked outside for a short while. I was thirsty but I was not going to leave now. I sat down again and picked up one of the many Bibles strewn around. I had never really read the Bible. I had it sprouted to me over several years when I was growing up. Father Nightingale said that Jesus himself had written most of the Bible. This wasn't true, but if it made Nightingale happy then it was okay by me.

Father Nightingale was a big man. He told me he was a big man. I was a little man. I was actually taller than him; so I never understood what he meant. He wore glasses and had a nose that comes from drinking sherry. He played golf and attended soccer matches. He didn't seem to do any holy things but he was the parish priest for Farley Hill. He was always called in for the last rites. He did a good last rites. He knew it off by heart. I heard him do Mrs. Gibson. She died of being tired. She was always tired. They probably have names for all those things now but to us kids she had just had enough. Nightingale's best last rites was Mr. Macinerny. Old Mac wasn't dead. He was dead drunk but still alive. Father Nightingale had just finished when Mac opened his eyes and vomited like a fountain all over him.

I was getting worried. Maybe the young nun had gotten sidetracked. I wasn't sure what I would do once I had returned the letter to Sister Lucy. I hadn't really made any plans. I was originally going back to Rome but there was nothing for me there now. I needed to visit New York and sort out my affairs. I thought about Rebecca. She was sweet. I knew I was falling in love with her, but what of her religious beliefs and aspirations? I couldn't see an RI teacher living with a crook. She knew all about me. I was sure that she wouldn't want me to stay around. I reminded myself of her beautiful recollections of the young seers' story. She told it with such conviction. She could have been one of the children herself, such was her passion. What had happened all those years ago? How do three children have such an experience? There was a statue of the Virgin Mary just to the side of me. I looked at the purity in the face. I looked at the man Jesus, nailed to a cross above the altar, and tried to imagine the pain. Around the side of the church were the Stations of the Cross. The pictures tell the story of the last punishing moments of the life of Jesus. Everyone con-demned the man. Who was he? He didn't write books or leave grand letters. The Vatican claimed to represent him. They built the church they claimed he wanted. The leader of the Catholic church was also at times the leader of a great army. How could they claim to be the house of God while slaughtering their foe? I thought about the files I had read in London. The Vatican had assisted the Nazis. They believed that communism was a greater threat than any Adolph Hitler posed. Could they really justify their actions by this?

I was leaning forward with my head resting in my hands, almost falling asleep, when a voice startled me.

"You have something for me."

It made me jump and I had a huge rush of adrenaline. My guest was already seated next to me. The side of her face was almost hidden by her traditional nun's attire, but I was in no doubt as to whom this person was.

CHAPTER 23

The church was peaceful. There were no more visitors. I could hear my own heart beating and my head was racing with ideas about what to say. She was controlling me with her silence, looking at me, looking away and turning back again. I wanted to say many things but said nothing. She sat majestic like, with her hands linked together resting on her lap. I really don't know what I had expected. Did I think I was going to conduct an interview with questions about Fatima, hearing tales about visions and miracles? I placed my hand inside my jacket pocket and withdrew the same pouch that I had used in Tuy. I gently unzipped it, carefully removing the two pieces of notepaper before turning to offer them to Sister Lucy. I had read so much about Lucia and now here she was sitting next to me, the woman and the child together.

Almost casually Sister Lucy took the pages from me. She gently kissed the folded paper and without sighting the text, placed the two sheets into a pocket in the front of her robe. We sat silent for a moment before she said, "You are a good man. The Blessed Virgin is very happy." Sister Lucy had a good command of English and her voice was eloquent. I desperately wanted to ask her questions and I was sure that she knew this.

She told me that she had something for me. She said it was worth more to her than anything she had have ever owned. She took a small object out of her pocket, took a hold of my hand, and placed her hand in mine. A small medal fell into my palm. The medallion had the image of Our Lady on one side and a small inscription on the other: to Jacinta, love Lucia. "I gave her this a few weeks before she died. It was to be for her 10th birthday but she was not to see this day." She paused and wiped the corner of her eye. "Jacinta's mother gave it back to me at the funeral." Sister Lucy recalled this with some sadness. I gave a promise that I would always look after this gift. I realised that Sister Lucy had tried to exchange something of equal value for the return of her letter. I would accept it for now but I would return it to her later.

Sister Lucy relaxed back into the timber pew. There were small cushions sitting randomly along the seat and I took one that lay beside me and offered it to her. She took the cushion but only held it to herself as though consoling someone. I sensed that she wanted to talk. I don't know quite what I believed before this meeting, but I was sure that this women was saintly. I was certain of that.

As a 10 year old child Lucia had been given a message, which contained a prophecy that she had since witnessed and another that I pray I never live to see. I wondered how an innocent child could be told of such a catastrophic event. The postscript to the note that Rebecca had copied for me told Sister Lucy that I had her original letter and that I was waiting at the church of Saint Dominique.

We remained seated together for a few more minutes before Sister Lucy indicated that she was about to leave. If she did have questions of me they were not going to be asked. She said, "I must return now...I have work." All I could think about was how this woman's entire life was one long continuous devotion, teaching, praying, and caring for people since the time she was just a child. She stood and blessed herself as she looked lovingly at the crucifix above the altar. I stood and made the sign of the cross. She took my hand and placed both of her hands around mine. This woman looked strong and resolute. I could sense the spirit of a young child and I smiled when I noticed that she still had thick eyebrows that joined. The young Lucia was said to have been very conscious and much bothered by her bushy eyebrows but Sister Lucy would have had no such vanity. With one final grasp of my hand she turned and moved to the end of the aisle. Her age did not prevent her from performing a perfect curtsy. I followed her to the rear of the church where I offered my arm as she took the two steps to street level. I asked her if I might accompany her back to the convent. She said that she would prefer it if she could walk back alone. She turned away, taking a few paces towards the footpath before stopping.

"Fatima," she said, turning back to face me. "We shall see each other in Fatima." She turned back towards the pavement and walked off towards the convent.

I hadn't realized that it was almost the 13th October, the anniversary of the Miracle of Fatima. I remembered the photograph I'd seen on the back of the flyer that I had picked up at my hotel in Coimbra. It showed a massive crowd rejoicing in the memory of the Miracle. I thought it would be great to see Sister Lucy in her hometown before her adoring supporters. I was sure I could talk Rebecca into going to Fatima with me. I couldn't wait to see her and tell her about my meeting with Sister Lucy.

I was so relieved that the letter was now finally in the rightful hands and hadn't become a mere trinket for Gelli. He may have wanted to wreak revenge on me for not delivering the letter to him or his cronies, but I didn't care. I thought of Maria. She had done nothing that I hadn't done myself a hundred times. She may have even hated being intimate with me but did so under instructions. I would never know if she had any real feelings for me and I was sure that day that I didn't care. I wanted to move on.

CHAPTER 24

Rebecca was excited that I was going to Fatima. She had decided to go weeks earlier after reading that Sister Lucy would lead the procession. It turned out that Sister Lucy had only attended the anniversary on a few occasions, so this really was going to be a special event. The festival day arrived and Rebecca suggested that we leave early because of the large crowds expected in Fatima. We took Rebecca's car as I had returned my rental some days earlier. We took our time and enjoyed the scenery.

Portugal is a great kaleidoscope of landscapes. Rolling mountains, flat grasslands and misty hills, followed by sun baked cork trees, olive groves and the Atlantic beaches. We passed through quaint little villages with flower-covered balconies, whitewashed houses and roofs of orange tiles. The villages all looked alike with narrow cobblestone streets and surrounded by Moorish walls. Rebecca gave me the history of each place we passed. Her understanding of Portuguese history was mainly from a religious perspective but she also knew plenty of the local culture and customs. I was finally playing tourist again and so happy to be with Rebecca.

Eventually our speed dropped to no more than a snail's pace. We had joined a queue that stretched for miles in front of us. There were many tour buses, people on bikes, hikers by the roadside and more and more cars. We were still several miles from the town but motorists were already leaving their cars parked on the side of the road or driving them into fields. There would be tens of thousands in Fatima that day. We decided to join the throng and park in a nearby field. The local farmer was very enterprising, charging a modest fee to gain entrance to his paddock. We set off and joined what had already become a procession.

The town centre of Fatima was packed. It was only 2pm but already difficult to move around the sidewalks. There was a great buzz of excitement and no sign of impatience from any groups. Rebecca and I queued for some time to get a drink and something to eat. We found a spot where we could sit in the car park of the Basilica, and ate our lunch. The Basilica in Fatima is vast and its forecourt larger than the Vatican. There is car parking for hundreds of cars and bays for scores of buses that arrive each year for the festival. Hospices and convents have sprung up in the shadow of the Basilica and inevitably, the fame of Fatima has resulted in its commercialisation. Restaurants abounded and were packed with pilgrims.

Inside the main church are the bodies of Francisco and Jacinta Marto. The children were originally buried near their home but it was felt that the Basilica offered a more fitting resting place. Even during the low season with no organized festivals thousands still pay their respects to the two children. Rebecca told me that there would normally be a midnight procession to celebrate the anniversary of the miracle but as Sister Lucy was taking part this year the organizers had decided to begin much earlier. The town looked different to me now than it had on my previous visit. There were portable bathroom facilities set up at various locations and stations for drinking water. The ground was hidden beneath a sea of people. Many of the pilgrims had already taken up vantage positions near the entrance to the church. We stood about mid-way and near what would become the centre aisle during the procession.

Over the next two hours the sea of people slowly formed ranks with hundreds of officials and volunteers on hand to help shape the crowd. By 6pm it was getting dark and a mass had begun on the main steps of the Basilica. The lights on the esplanade were switched on and the front of the church was illuminated. The crucifix on top of the Basilica lit up and shone brightly against the darkening skies. A voice came over the loudspeakers set up around the town centre and a request was made to light the candles. Rebecca and I lit ours and soon the centre of Fatima was a beautiful ocean of flickering lights. The voices of a giant children's choir rang forth and a great air of excitement filled the crowd.

I could hear the sound of hand bells ringing, and turned to see the processional group slowly making their way towards the church. Everyone had turned to see the large statue of the Blessed Virgin Mary at the head of the procession. The statue, which was laden with masses of white flowers, was being carried high on the shoulders of four men. As the statue passed by me I could hear faint applause coming from the rear of the crowd. It was for Sister Mary

Lucy. Local children flanked her on both sides and as she reached each section of the crowd they showed their appreciation by applauding and shouting words of devotion. As she approached the main body of the crowd people jostled for positions. We were standing on the edge of the main aisle.

Sister Lucy was soon level with us and as though seeking me out in this vast crowd she stopped at my position. The children accompanying her also stopped and waited as she moved towards me. Sister Lucy took my hand and after lifting her head skyward, leaned forward to gently kiss the back of my hand causing the people around me to fall completely silent. The attention had made me feel important but I was also embarrassed and hoped that the crowd didn't think I was some kind of holy man. Sister Lucy still clasping my hand said, "I give you this promise…if you have faith, you too will see." I didn't respond, but desperately wanted her to explain what she had meant.

By now the crowd had milled around us, and an official was making a space so that Sister Lucy could move back to the processional path. With the exception of Rebecca, the people around me would have had no idea why I had been singled out for this exchange. Sister Lucy had moved away leaving me to re-examine her words over and over. The applause became louder and soon the entire crowd was welcoming the woman who had spoken with Our Lady. The voices of the young choir became stronger and every soul had joined in the singing of The Lord's My Shepherd. Some sang in Portuguese, some in Italian, some in Latin, and some in languages I had never heard. The song was the same the world over and the people there that day were as one.

I turned to see that Rebecca was wiping away tears from her eyes. We kissed and embraced. I told her that I was so glad that we had met. We stood arm in arm candles raised and sang hymns together. The procession of priests and nuns followed by altar boys and local school children, continued for some time until all had settled at the entrance to the church. The front of the church had been converted into a large altar and the mass continued. A young local priest was conducting the mass aided by guest speakers for the various sermons. The general mass had passed quickly when the father called on the huge crowd to welcome Sister Mary Lucy. As she made her entrance from the side of the altar the crowd roared its approval. The applause lasted several minutes and it required the priest's pleas to have the crowd desist. Finally, the excited crowd became calm and people stood with hands to mouths and hearts. Sister Lucy held the crowd to ransom whilst she said a quiet prayer. Finally she was ready to address her adoring public. Sister Lucy spoke in her native tongue, whilst translations were provided in several other languages.

"The Blessed Virgin Mary is very happy that so many peoples continue to come to this place to show their love and devotion to her immaculate heart. She asks me to implore you all to put pressure on your church leaders to take heed of the message that she gave to me and my beloved friends Francisco and Jacinta Marto. Our Lady of Fatima has told us how to save Christianity and how we can be spared from horrible wars and communist slavery. The church must act on these requests. She also gave to me a final message, which I have asked the Holy Fathers of Rome to reveal to you, her beloved followers. She is sad that this has still not taken place. It is not a message for you the peoples to follow but a message for which the holy church must respond. It is their words that the Blessed Virgin Mary wishes for you all to hear. The message of Fatima is more important today than at any time in the past. I promise to you now that I will continue to seek support from all members of the Catholic church and hope that one day soon we can all hear the response from Rome. Finally I would like to remind you all of the most important part of the message given to the world that day. In the end, my immaculate heart will triumph."

With this a fantastic roar of approval came from the crowd, which later estimates put at 200,000 strong. The choir began to sing and the priest did his best to end the mass in an orderly fashion but the crowd was high. The procession began again with the image of Our Lady gaining more rapturous cheers as it passed through the crowd. School children handed out little booklets containing the message of Fatima and the nuns handed out rosary beads, blessed during the mass. The evening had been a huge success and the outpouring of peace from the massive crowd was truly overwhelming.

CHAPTER 25

The funeral had been very tough for both of us. I helped carry his little white coffin to where he would be laid to rest while a friend supported Rebecca, who I felt sure would collapse. The cemetery was beautifully maintained and the grass in the infants section, a perfect green carpet. Our friends stood back, which made the service very intimate. The priest said some nice words and I recited a small verse, which I had written. Before the body was lowered I placed a small envelope onto the coffin. Inside I had placed a photograph of all three of us together, and a note, which read, "In this Marble Orchard the trees will be forever green, they will give shade to you and to all the other roses. Love mummy and daddy." I scooped up some soil and let it gently cascade downward and I watched as it landed on the little white casket, covering my dreams.

I visit the cemetery often but prefer to be alone. Rebecca visits by herself too. She doesn't tell me but I know. I gave her some flowers recently for her birthday, only to find them on Justin's grave a day or so later. We were lucky enough to have more children and Rebecca combines motherhood with teaching. Her life is full and she seems content and happy. I kept secret those final seconds on the 7th floor. I was so distressed at losing my boy that I must have become delusional for a moment.

I saw a light more intense than the sun and yet I could look directly into it. I was frightened but I didn't move away. I looked at Rebecca, her head still resting on the child. The image of a lady appeared. She spoke to me. "The child will be with me, you will see him again…you must have faith." As she lifted Justin, the brilliant light faded and the room turned cold and grey. Rebecca hadn't moved, her head still resting on our boy.

Brian Dullaghan
PO Box 1148
Ashfield, NSW 2131
Australia
Email:
info@briandullaghan.com

0-595-33957-3

Printed in the United States
27853LVS00005B/39